"Do you think it is wise for us to do this?"

"Probably not," Perry admitted, "but I have to know why you deserted me."

"That period of our life is over, and it isn't wise to rake up painful memories…." Her lips trembled as she pressed a hand against them. "But I do want to spend time with you, Perry."

An eager light flickered in Perry's black eyes, filling Lorene with conflicting emotions. Apprehension swept over her. If Perry wanted to resume their previous relationship, did she have the willpower to resist him? Did she want to?

Books by Irene Brand

Love Inspired

Child of Her Heart #19
Heiress #37
To Love and Honor #49
A Groom To Come Home To #70
Tender Love #95
The Test of Love #114
Autumn's Awakening #129
Summer's Promise #148
Love at Last #190

IRENE BRAND

Writing has been a lifelong interest of this author, who says that she started her first novel when she was eleven years old and hasn't finished it yet. However, since 1984, she's published twenty-four contemporary and historical novels and three nonfiction titles with publishers such as Zondervan, Thomas Nelson, Barbour and Kregel. She started writing professionally in 1977 after she completed her master's degree in history at Marshall University. Irene taught in secondary public schools for twenty-three years, but retired in 1989 to devote herself to writing.

Consistent involvement in the activities of her local church has been a source of inspiration for Irene's work. Traveling with her husband, Rod, to forty-nine of the United States—Hawaii excepted—and to thirty-two foreign countries has also inspired her writing. Irene is grateful to the many readers who have written to say that her inspiring stories and compelling portrayals of characters with strong faith have made a positive impression on their lives. You can write to her at P.O. Box 2770, Southside, WV 25187 or visit her Web site at http://www.irenebrand.com.

Love at Last
Irene Brand

Love Inspired®

Published by Steeple Hill Books™

STEEPLE HILL BOOKS

Steeple
Hill™

ISBN 0-373-87197-X

LOVE AT LAST

Visit us at www.steeplehill.com

Printed in U.S.A.

"I, even I, am He
who blots out your transgressions, for My own
sake, and remembers your sins no more."
—*Isaiah* 43:25

Thanks to my friend Jason Duncan
for sharing his football expertise with me.

Chapter One

As Lorene Harvey walked across the campus of Woodston College, she was tempted to turn tail and run. The redbrick buildings, the shaded avenues and the memorial fountain, cascading colorful rainbows in the sweltering summer heat, brought unwelcome thoughts—memories of two years of her life she'd tried in vain to forget.

She hadn't wanted to come to this Kentucky town in the first place, and the sudden surge of best-forgotten incidents confirmed her opinion that coming to Woodston had been a mistake. Would she ever put the past behind her? Why couldn't she blot out recollections of twenty years ago when she'd made the biggest error of her life? A mistake that had spawned an empty vacuum where her heart ought to be.

But Lorene hadn't established a successful media-relations business by surrendering to her mistakes. She paused before the splashing fountain, determined to suppress her regrets of days gone by. After a few minutes she took a deep breath, forced a pleasant smile and walked into the administration building.

Following the signs to room 202, she tapped lightly on the open door and entered. The receptionist, who looked to be in her sixties, smiled and said pleasantly, "May I help you?"

"I want to see the vice chair of Woodston's bicentennial commission. I understand this is his office."

The secretary's eyes expressed caution. "He might not have time to see you. May I have your name?"

Lorene's smile remained, but her jaw tightened and her gray-green eyes flashed like summer lightning, and in a harsh, uncompromising voice that didn't sound like her usual velvet tones, she said, "I'm Lorene Harvey of Tri-State Public Relations Agency in Pittsburgh. I've been in Woodston for two hours trying to find someone to talk to me about the historical celebration our firm is supposed to promote. Mr. Kincaid, chairman of the commission, isn't available, and I was sent here."

Lorene was aware that a door had opened behind her, but without turning she said, "If everybody in this town is too busy to talk to me, our firm is too busy to represent Woodston." Turning toward the door, she added, "We'll return the retainer Mr. Kincaid sent us."

"I—I'm sorry," the receptionist stammered. Her face flushed, and her eyes darted to a point over Lorene's shoulder.

"I'll talk to you, Lorene."

The voice jolted Lorene out of her anger, and she whirled to stare at the man standing in the doorway of the adjoining office. She took a sharp breath and her pulse raced.

As if Lorene's surprise appearance hadn't dealt his vulnerability a near-fatal blow, Perry Saunders continued, "You'll have to forgive Alma—she's overprotective of me. Come in." He motioned toward his office.

Lorene's yearning eyes swept his beautifully proportioned body from the neatly shod feet to his extraordinary eyes, as dark as black onyx, to the thick silvery-gray hair that fell loosely over his forehead before it tapered neatly to the collar of his dark business suit. Stunned by this unexpected encounter, she was powerless to do anything except nod and move toward him. Tense fingers tightened on the handle of her briefcase as she walked on trembling legs into a comfortable room with high ceilings, long, heavily draped windows and modern oak office furnishings.

Perry closed the door and, thinking her legs might not support her much longer, Lorene dropped quickly to a couch at the left of the desk. She looked upward and slowly studied each feature of the face that, except in her dreams, she hadn't seen for twenty years. Perry had a long, lean face, high cheekbones and a straight, prominent nose. Except for the gray hair, she couldn't see that he'd aged at all. The last time she'd seen Perry, his hair had been jet-black.

"I've always wondered what you'd look like with gray hair," she said evenly, proud of herself that the emotional shock of seeing him wasn't evident in her voice.

Perry's neat gray mustache framed a sensitive, well-shaped mouth that widened into a smile. Sitting beside Lorene, he took her hand, and his eyes hungrily scanned each of her features. Thick dark hair fell gracefully over shapely shoulders, and her eyes of gray and green shades glowed with wonder and surprise at meeting him again. Lorene was tall and well proportioned with a slender waist, no heavier than she'd been when she was twenty. She looked just as he remembered—generously curved lips, delicate bone structure, dainty nose and long black eyelashes that splayed over rosy skin. She wore black dress pants, a red blazer and black pumps rather than the jeans and sweatshirts she'd preferred when he'd known her.

The most profound difference was in her character. In her teens, Lorene had been insecure, possessing low self-esteem, mostly because she had a domineering father who wouldn't give her the freedom to think for herself. It was apparent that the years had brought an inner strength that hadn't lessened her determination or marred her delicate beauty.

Lorene squirmed under his intense scrutiny, and he said lightly, "No gray in *your* hair, I see."

"Thanks to my beautician," she admitted with a slight smile. Then surprise and disbelief overspread her face, and she cried out, "You're teaching in a Christian college! What happened to your engineering studies?"

"I finished my engineering degree, but I later went to seminary, received my doctorate in Bible studies ten years ago and came to teach in Woodston."

She wanted to ask why he'd changed his profession. Instead she said, "I'm sorry I lost my temper with your secretary, but I still intend to return the retainer the commission sent and be on my way."

Perry tightened his grip on her hand and said quickly, "When I've wondered for years where you were, do you think I'll let you walk out of my life again? Tell me what disturbed you this afternoon. Most people consider Woodston a friendly town."

"At Mr. Kincaid's bank I was passed from one employee to another until a secretary told me he wasn't available this afternoon and sent me here. She said that the vice chair of the commission was at this office. She didn't mention your name, and by that time I was too annoyed to ask."

"If you'd known I was the one you were to see, would you have come?"

The question was as sharp as a knife wound in her heart. She lowered her head. When she didn't know the answer herself, how could she respond? She was suddenly overcome with an uncontrollable urge to leave this town. She'd run away from Perry once before, and she had even more reason to leave him now. Standing, she pulled her hand from his.

"No, Perry, I wouldn't have. I'll refund the deposit to the bicentennial commission and leave. You'll be able to find another public relations firm closer to Woodston. I don't know why we were contacted in the first place."

With an indulgent smile, Perry said, "Mr. Kincaid has political ambitions, and he thought if he hired a nationally known PR firm, he might gain out-of-state recognition."

Inching toward the door, Lorene said, "I'll recommend a good company in Louisville that can provide as much publicity as my firm can."

She had her hand on the doorknob, but Perry moved in front of the door and barred her exit.

"Lorene," Perry said as he softly cupped her chin with his warm hand and lifted her face so that their eyes met and gazes held. "I'm not concerned with Woodston receiving national recognition." There was a look of unflinching determination on his face. "But I do care about *us*. You walked out on me once, and I've never forgotten the emptiness that caused in my life." His voice became pleading in its intensity. "It's okay if you don't want to represent Woodston, but stay a few days for *me*. I think you owe me that much.''

She closed her eyes against the entreaty in his voice, her heart aching with pain. Did he think he was the only one who'd been hurt? And he had no idea how much she did owe him! Would she ever tell him? Lorene's heart and emotions demanded that she stay in Woodston, but her intellect shouted that she should put the past behind her as quickly as she could. She'd built a life without Perry Saunders. Besides, if he knew the secret she harbored, he wouldn't want her to stay.

His hand slid over her cheek in a wistful gesture and Lorene opened her eyes. The moment of decision was crucial. A familiar smile hovered in Perry's dark eyes, and in spite of the warning that hammered in her brain, Lorene nodded tensely. ''Well, I'm not staying a few days, but we can talk for a few hours.''

Perry's heart warmed when she yielded to his pleading, though he was instantly sorry he'd asked her to stay. His life wasn't his own anymore. When he'd committed to full-time Christian service, Perry had repudiated his love for Lorene. Would being with her again distract him from his chosen profession? He didn't know, but he was happy that his prayers had been answered. Humorously, he thought that God might have gotten tired of his entreaties. Not a day had passed since she'd left him that Perry hadn't asked God to take care of Lorene and allow him to see her again.

Lorene moved toward the chair in front of his desk, but he said, "Let's sit on the couch where it's more comfortable. I'll have Alma bring us something to drink. Coffee?"

She wasn't keen about sitting beside him, but she moved to the maroon leather couch and answered, "That will be fine. I take it black."

"Yes, I remember."

He turned on the intercom, gave the order and joined her at a discreet distance on the couch. Now that she'd gotten over her initial surprise at seeing Perry, Lorene had her emotions under control, and she was eager to find out what he'd been doing, too.

When Alma entered with a tray and placed it on the low table in front of them, Lorene smiled at her and said, "I'm not usually so short-tempered, and I apologize for my rudeness. I know it isn't ethical to break the verbal contract our company made with Woodston, so I'll not back out of our agreement. But since I've gotten off on the wrong foot already, I'll send another representative to work with the commission."

A pleasant smile lighted Alma's face, transforming her rather plain features. "Professor Saunders is chairman of his department, and many salesmen and others drop in to chat when he's busy. I try to steer people away when I can, but I do get carried away sometimes. I had no idea who you were. Mr. Cranston was the initial contact from your agency."

Lorene sipped gratefully on the hot beverage

Alma had poured. "Kenneth Cranston accepted another job quite suddenly and didn't give me any advance notice. My other employees are busy elsewhere, so it was up to me. But I shouldn't have let my anger at Cranston govern my attitude toward Woodston. Forgive me?"

"Certainly," Alma said as she left the office, closing the door behind her, but not before her eyes shifted appraisingly from Perry to Lorene.

"Alma had been the secretary to my predecessor, and she has a tendency to mother me. I have a standing invitation to her house for dinner every Sunday, or any other time I want a home-cooked meal."

Concluding from his comments that he lived alone, Lorene glanced at his left hand. No ring on the third finger. Her heart fluttered slightly at the implication and her fingers tightened on the coffee cup. "You aren't married?"

"No."

She met his eyes briefly, but lowered her gaze when he continued, "You don't have a ring, either. Why?"

"That's a question I've often asked myself," Lorene admitted, "but I've never come up with a satisfactory answer." Her eyes clouded with memories of the past, and Perry moved toward her.

"Mr. Kincaid wants to see you," Alma said over the intercom, breaking the tension between them. The door opened immediately and a thin beanpole of a man barged into the office.

"Are you Miss Harvey?" he said, coming toward Lorene with outstretched hand.

Perry cupped Lorene's elbow and helped her to stand.

"Lorene Harvey, meet Gaston Kincaid, chairman of Woodston's bicentennial commission."

"I'm sorry I wasn't on hand to meet you," Kincaid said, pumping her hand. "I contacted the bank by phone and learned you were in town. I'd received the e-mail message that you were replacing Cranston, but I didn't know when to expect you. I trust Professor Saunders has taken care of you."

Perry flushed slightly, but Lorene answered smoothly, "I've only been here a short time, and we haven't gotten around to discussing the PR agenda."

"I have an engagement tonight," Kincaid said, "but I'll notify the commission members that we'll meet tomorrow evening. Perry can give you a file outlining our plans, or do you have what we sent Cranston?"

"Unfortunately, Kenneth deleted his records from our computer system before he left. But I can read through the file tonight and look around town tomorrow. Perhaps you and I should have a private conference before the meeting?"

"I'm a very busy man, so I can't give you much of my time," Kincaid said, "but Perry can help you. Will you take Miss Harvey out for dinner tonight?"

"It will be a pleasure. Since the fall quarter has

started, my schedule is flexible. I'll give Miss Harvey all the help I possibly can."

"Good! Good!" Kincaid said, and hustled out of the office with an abrupt wave of his hand. Shaking his head, Perry moved to close the door.

"Kincaid is one of the college trustees, and he twisted my arm to serve on the celebration commission." With a slight grimace, he added, "His first priority is promoting himself and his business, and then he turns the rest of his attention to steering the course of this college. He has his good points, but he can be overbearing."

He sat beside her again. "Now, where were we?"

The phone rang, and with a look of annoyance Perry picked up the receiver on his desk and answered. He concluded that call, started back to the couch and the phone rang again. Perry's handsome features faded into a frown when he took the second call. What was the matter with Alma? She usually held all calls when he was in a conference. Was she deliberately interrupting his conversation with Lorene? It must have been obvious to her that they knew each other. He didn't need Alma's interference in his attempt to prevent Lorene's immediate departure from Woodston.

"We'll never manage any privacy here," Perry said when he finished that conversation, "so we'll talk this evening over dinner. I prefer a restaurant out of town. If we stay in Woodston, we'll meet too many people who know me and want to visit."

Lorene knew it wasn't prudent to have dinner with Perry, but she'd seldom displayed any caution in her relationship with him.

She looked at her watch. "I'll enjoy having dinner with you. After all," she added with a grin, "Mr. Kincaid practically ordered you to entertain me. It may take quite a while to go over Woodston's plans, but I can work late tonight."

"Where are you staying?"

"At Riverview Ridge, the B and B on the outskirts of town. My travel agency gave it a four-star rating. The apartment I'm renting is in the back wing, facing the river."

"You made a good choice. I'll pick you up at six-thirty."

Already having second thoughts, Lorene panicked at the thought of spending an evening alone with Perry. "Do you think it's wise for us to do this?"

"Probably not," he admitted honestly, "but I have to know why you deserted me. It's weighed on my mind for years."

"That period of our life is over, so maybe we shouldn't rake up painful memories that won't do either of us any good, but…" Her lips trembled and she pressed a hand against them. "But I do want to spend some time with you, Perry. I'll be ready." She gave him her cell phone number. "Let me know if you change your mind."

"I won't change my mind."

An eager light flickered in Perry's black eyes, filling Lorene with conflicting emotions. Apprehension swept over her, and she knew she should cancel this dinner. If Perry wanted to resume their previous relationship, did she have the willpower to resist him? Or did she even want to resist?

Chapter Two

Traveling toward Riverview Ridge, Lorene knew that she should find someone else to take this assignment. She pulled to the curb of a tree-shaded street and telephoned her office. After talking with several members of her staff, she conceded that it was impossible for anyone else from the agency to come to Woodston for several weeks. She had two choices—back out on the firm's commitment to Woodston or stay and handle the promotion herself. Accepting the inevitable, she drove on.

If she had to stay in Woodston for two months, Lorene was pleased that she'd have a comfortable place to live. When she'd checked in at the B and B earlier in the day, she'd been delighted with her choice. The white frame 1850s story-and-a-half cottage had enormous ivy-covered redbrick chimneys. The house was T-shaped, with dormer windows set in the front and rear sections of the main structure's roof. A small front porch was in Queen Anne style, and a long screened-in back porch extended the full length of the stem part of the building. Green shutters graced the long, narrow windows on the first floor.

The entrance to the two-room apartment was through a private door on the back porch and up narrow, steep steps. According to the proprietor, Dottie Montgomery, this had once been the caretaker's quarters, but she'd had it renovated into an apartment. The Montgomerys also had three single rooms in the main part of the house for rent. But Lorene needed space to accommodate her computer and other office equipment she'd brought with her.

Dottie Montgomery, a buxom, hospitable blonde in her mid-sixties, met Lorene on the porch with a glass of lemonade in her hand. Pointing to a round table circled by three chairs, the landlady set the lemonade on the table and said, "Sit down and rest a spell. I'll have my husband carry up your things. Climbing those steps can get tiresome when you're loaded down with suitcases."

But Dottie seemed to be talkative, and right now Lorene was in no mood for visiting. What she really wanted to do was to go somewhere, scream at the top of her voice and release the pent-up frustration that had been burgeoning through the deepest recesses of her being since she'd encountered Perry two hours ago. In her present frame of mind, she worried that she couldn't be polite to Dottie, so she said, "Thank you, but I'll need to settle in to my apartment and get ready to start working tomorrow." She took a deep swig of the lemonade. "That really is delicious. Thank you."

"You gonna eat dinner here? I serve breakfast and dinner."

"Not tonight. Perry Saunders, cochair of the bicentennial commission, is taking me out for dinner so we can discuss plans for the celebration. And I'll prepare my own breakfast, too. My working hours will be irregular, so I'll notify you on a day-to-day basis when I want to eat dinner with you. Will that be satisfactory?"

"Whatever makes our visitors happy suits us," Dottie said. "My husband, John, and I are here to make your stay comfortable, so let us know if there's anything we can do to help you. We're both involved in the bicentennial celebration, so we'll be seeing you often."

Taking another swallow of the lemonade, Lorene said, "I'll bring my luggage into the porch, and you can send it up when it's convenient."

Lorene retrieved three suitcases and two garment bags from her late-model station wagon and put them on the porch. She brought in a small file cabinet. Then she carried her laptop and cosmetic case with her as she went upstairs to the homelike apartment.

The combination living room and kitchenette had

a fireplace with a beautiful, hand-carved mantel. The interior woodwork of the house was all original. White crocheted doilies dressed up the ancient tables, plump pillows were piled on the couch and a handmade quilt covered the bed. A gable window looked out over a pleasant expanse of field that led down to the Ohio River a quarter of a mile away.

Riverview Ridge was a quaint building, and Lorene had promptly decided that spending some time here would be almost like a vacation. But now that she'd met Perry, she couldn't even be excited about this apartment, which was casually furnished in antiques that would have sold for a small fortune in Pittsburgh.

Lorene laid her things in the small, low-ceilinged bedroom, kicked off her shoes and lounged on the soft sofa, a concession to modern comfort among the ancient pieces of furniture. She laid an arm over her closed eyes as her tortured mind recalled the past.

She'd met Perry Saunders when they were both college sophomores. They had several classes together and became good friends. Their friendship slowly developed into a beautiful romance. Although they were very much in love, they couldn't afford to get married, for Lorene's parents threatened to cut off her tuition money if she married Perry. Both of them were Christians and opposed to sex before marriage, but in a weak moment they succumbed to the intense magnetism building between them and made love once.

Afterward, they agreed it wouldn't happen again, and both of them welcomed the summer break, thinking it might dull the flame that smoldered in their hearts. As part of his engineering studies, Perry would be on field assignment in Mexico for three months. That time of separation would give them time to put their love in perspective with their goals for the future.

But unforeseen circumstances ruined their plans. Her family moved to another town that summer and after being ill for almost a year, Lorene continued her education at another school. She'd had no news of Perry until she saw him today. It had taken years to numb the pain of losing him, and just seeing him for an hour had flooded her mind with pleasant memories and past disappointments.

After Lorene left his office, Perry lowered his head to his hands. *God, thank You for answering my prayers and bringing her back into my life, but now that she's here, I don't know what to do with her. Should we take up where we left off? I believe You meant us for each other, but just like Abraham and Sarah in the Bible, we didn't wait for Your timing. We took matters into our own hands, and that never works out. God, I need Your direction now more than I've ever needed it.*

He remembered the time he'd given Lorene a

promise ring, held her in his arms and whispered, "I love you with all my heart, and I want to marry you as soon as I possibly can. God made us for each other, and I'll never marry any woman except you."

His love had deepened and intensified every day they'd been together. When she'd left him and eventually disappeared from his life, Perry was so distressed that at one point he'd contemplated suicide. He had telephoned her home repeatedly but she didn't return his calls. He wrote letters, which she didn't answer, and when he went to her home, he learned the family had moved. He finally gave up, believing that she no longer wanted him.

When despair had almost conquered him, when he was at the lowest ebb, he'd experienced God's call to full-time Christian service. He'd believed that God was giving him a new life to replace the one he'd envisioned with Lorene, by leading him into the field of Christian education.

Perry considered his promise to Lorene as binding as if he'd made it before a minister, so he'd lived a celibate life, denying himself the pleasure of wife and family. It was years before he could attend a wedding without experiencing a pain in his heart that gnawed at his innards until he was physically sick.

Today, when he'd heard Lorene's voice in the office, he'd known immediately who it was, and when he'd seen her, he'd been as physically aware of her as if they'd separated only yesterday.

Considering the tingle of excitement that had surged through him when she'd delayed her departure from Woodston long enough to have dinner with him, Perry wondered if he'd done the right thing in encouraging her to stay. When she'd abandoned him twenty years ago without any explanation, it was obvious she hadn't loved him. If she stayed at Woodston until after the big celebration, he'd be seeing her often. Would his love for her surface again? Grimly he determined that wouldn't happen. He couldn't risk being rejected a second time.

Lorene stirred when she heard a knock at the door. She padded across the hardwood floor in her stocking feet and opened the door for the landlord to carry in her luggage.

"Hope you'll be comfortable here, Lorene," John Montgomery said. "If I can be any help, let me know."

"This is a beautiful home. Has it been in your family long?"

His laugh was slow and hearty. "No. Dottie and I bought the property several years ago. The place had been vacant for a long time, and it took us three years to fix it up. It's a good project to bring in a little money and keep us out of devilment in our retirement years."

"It's a nice location—should be quiet at night."

"Sure is." He tipped the brim of his cap, a gesture that she'd seen several times already in Woodston, perhaps a custom left over from the Old South. "Make yourself at home."

She closed the door after John's departure, went into the bedroom and spread out on the canopied bed that would have been at home in *Gone with the Wind*. At six o'clock Lorene forced herself to get up and check out her wardrobe. Leaving most of her luggage where John had placed it, she opened a garment bag and chose a white button-front, long-sleeved, lined crochet sweater and a long patterned skirt that swirled gracefully around her ankles when she walked. She eased her feet into white sandals and crossed the hall to the bathroom.

Wedged in behind the staircase, the bathroom contained a shower stall and the other necessities. Lorene brushed her hair and repaired her makeup, giving special attention to her eyes, hoping to camouflage the raw hurt and deep longing that hadn't been there when she'd stood before the mirror earlier in the day. She didn't believe the makeup did any good, for the eyes staring back at her still had a bleak and wary expression.

From her jewelry box she took the silver ring set with a small garnet that Perry had given her when he'd promised to love her forever. Promise rings had been popular on campus between engaged couples, and Perry had saved for weeks before he'd accumulated enough money to buy the ring.

Lorene slipped the ring on her finger, but quickly

took it off and dropped it back in the box. She fastened diamond solitaires in her ears and clamped the jewelry box tight.

Since Perry might not know how to access her apartment, she went to the porch to wait for him. But he must have been familiar with Riverview Ridge, because he drove in and parked beside her station wagon before she had time to sit down. He came toward her, dressed in a red sport shirt and black trousers, looking like the young man she remembered. Until she'd encountered him today, Lorene had never seen Perry in a suit and tie.

"Ready?" he asked.

"Yes. I thought you might not know how to find me, so I came downstairs to wait," she explained, not wanting him to think she'd been so eager for this dinner date.

"Dottie only has one apartment, so I knew where you were. We don't have many sleeping accommodations in town, and sometimes I have to recommend a lodging place to college visitors. I've made it my business to know what's available."

"Then you know what an interesting apartment it is."

"Interesting, and comfortable, I believe."

Perry drove a new blue sedan. Remembering the days when he'd used a bicycle for transportation around campus, Lorene was pleased that the years had brought him prosperity.

"What kind of food do you prefer tonight?" he

asked as they left Woodston's city limits. "I'm going across the river to Indiana, where there's a choice of fine eating places." His lips curved in an infectious smile. "Always before when we ate out, I couldn't afford anything except pizza and burgers. I'd like to buy something better for you tonight."

Was this going to be a night of recalling what they'd once shared? Lorene wondered.

"I still like pizza and burgers," Lorene assured him, grinning. "But you choose. I enjoy most foods."

"Then we'll go to a family restaurant with a wide selection of entrées. Now, tell me about yourself. What have you been up to since we were together? You're apparently doing all right, since you have your own business."

"I finished college in New Jersey, and I worked in several PR agencies around the country for a few years. I couldn't find any town that suited me until I settled in Pittsburgh eight years ago. I went into partnership with an elderly man, and when he retired, I was able to buy the business at a reasonable price."

"Are your parents well?"

"Yes. They live in Philadelphia, and I don't see them often. That's another reason I was disgruntled over having to come to Woodston. Our whole family gets together once a year when we vacation at the same place, and we had reservations in Atlantic City for the next two weeks. I had to cancel."

"I'm sorry about that. You could have delayed coming to Woodston."

Lorene shook her head. "That's business for you. When you're the boss, you have to be the troubleshooter, too. And it looks like I'll have to stay in Woodston. I made several phone calls and no one else will be available for a few weeks. I don't like to be away from the business for such a long period, but I have a reliable office manager."

Her words both delighted and disturbed Perry. How much togetherness could they experience without being swept headlong into their previous relationship? He struggled with an overwhelming desire to pull her close to him, and he didn't believe Lorene was insensitive to his presence, either. Her body was tense and her well-formed hands were clenched in her lap. He sensed she was fighting to maintain her composure, but her face was unyielding, as if she had no intention of allowing herself to surrender to the past.

Earlier today, he knew her determination had crumbled in her surprise at seeing him. For a moment she'd been lost in her emotions and her heart had bonded with his as eagerly as it had in their youth. He believed if he'd taken her in his arms then, she wouldn't have resisted. But she was in control now. With an inward sigh he realized that was just as well. Her willpower would encourage him to stifle yearnings he couldn't indulge.

"I'm sorry you have to stay when you don't want to."

She waved an expressive hand, and her body seemed to relax as they talked of impersonal matters.

"It's all in a day's work," she said, "but I feel as if I'm coming to Woodston in the dark. I picked up that file from Alma as I left your office, but I haven't looked at it yet. I'll try to study through it tomorrow."

The restaurant was located one block from a busy highway. Perry asked for a corner booth, so they were fairly well isolated. Soft music filtered through the room as they ate, muting their conversation from those around them. They spent almost two hours in the restaurant discussing their respective jobs, talking as friends. Lorene didn't want to open old wounds. Still, she couldn't help wonder if Perry no longer cared for her.

When they'd finished their dessert, Lorene said, "Since I'll have to take on the bicentennial project, are we going to admit that we used to know each other?"

Perry lifted his eyebrows in surprise. "Why not? It must have been obvious to Alma that we aren't strangers."

Lorene's fingers traced the pattern of the place mat. Without meeting his gaze, she said, "I need to know what to keep secret and what to say. I don't want to be an embarrassment to you."

"Why not say we were college friends and let it go at that?"

"That's fine with me," she said with a sinking heart, knowing that she'd long ago forfeited the right to be more than friends. "Seeing you was more than I bargained for when I came to Woodston."

"Maybe our meeting again is God's plan for us. Have you considered that?"

"Until I've atoned for my past sins, I can't expect God to be concerned over my welfare."

Unspoken pain turned Perry's eyes into inky, unfathomable orbs as he placed his hand over hers. "We don't have to make restitution for our sins to have God love us. He loved us enough to send Jesus to make atonement for us. God knows our hearts, and He forgave us for making a wrong choice." He paused, adding reminiscently, with some bitterness, "But it took a long time to forgive myself."

"Does that mean you're sorry for—" she hesitated a few seconds "—the months we dated?"

"We might be better off not to discuss what happened years ago, but since you've brought it up— you know as well as I do that I enjoyed *all* of our time together."

Remembering the outcome of their engagement revived a pain in Lorene's heart she found hard to bear. Her fingers stirred in his grasp and he released her hand.

"I'll mention to Mr. Kincaid and Alma that we knew each other in college. We had a lot of good times together, and I don't see why we can't be friends. We can't avoid each other while you're here.''

Perry's offer of friendship was rather like offering a starving person a teaspoon of chicken broth. But after she'd deserted him once, without an explanation, she'd relinquished the right to expect anything more.

When they returned to the car, Perry inserted his key in the ignition and started the engine. Memories of the past flashed through his mind, and he sat silently for a couple of minutes before he turned to Lorene.

"I shouldn't ask this, but I have to know. Why did you just drop me without an explanation? Why didn't you answer my letters or return my telephone calls?''

A startled gasp escaped her lips and she faced him quickly. She latched on to his second question, and he didn't seem to notice that she avoided the first one. "What telephone calls? What letters? When did you write to me?''

"I sent a dozen or so letters that summer I was in Mexico. Days would go by when we didn't have any communication with the outside world, but I mailed you a letter when I could. We went to a town every two or three weeks, and I always telephoned, but I couldn't contact you. Your parents told me you didn't want to talk to me, but I kept calling, hoping you'd answer the phone.''

Anger burned so fiercely in Lorene's heart that her voice sounded harsh and raspy. "I had no idea you'd tried to get in touch with me. That's why I allowed my father to convince me that you were glad to get rid of me."

"I should have known," Perry muttered. Her words cut like a flesh wound. "Your father never did approve of our relationship, but I can't understand why you wouldn't have expected me to write and why you didn't contact me."

"Our mail was delivered to a post-office box, and Dad always picked it up, so it was easy for them to intercept my messages. Perry, I'm so sorry. Leaving you was the worst mistake I've ever made, but I didn't have your address in Mexico, and I didn't want to take a chance on your parents mistakenly opening my mail. When I didn't hear from you, I thought what we'd done had turned you against me—that you didn't love me any longer."

"I gave you no reason to think that," he said sharply.

She steeled herself against the deep emotion in his voice. "I just can't believe my parents treated me that way."

"You don't believe me?"

"Of course I believe *you*. But they'd have saved me a lot of heartache if they'd stayed out of our private affairs."

"I finished the job training in time to start my senior year at college. I came to your home, intending to force my way in to see you, only to learn your family had moved. If your neighbors knew where you'd gone, they wouldn't tell me.''

Lorene unconsciously twisted her slender hands together and leaned her head against the window. She held back tears of rage and disappointment. She remembered vividly the despair of the months following her separation from Perry. Though her parents told her persistently that he'd deceived her, only pretending to love her until he'd violated her purity, Lorene continued to believe they were wrong. She pored over each day's mail, looking for a letter. Finally the day came when she no longer wanted to see Perry and lived in dread that he would come back to her. But she'd never forgotten how much she loved him, and her parents had never completely convinced Lorene that he *hadn't* loved her.

He tenderly caressed her cheek with a knuckle and stroked the long hair on her shoulder.

''I'm sorry I've distressed you. It's my fault. I should have known you wouldn't walk out on me. It's all right. Don't let it ruin your evening.''

Chapter Three

Reluctant to part with Lorene for the night, Perry drove westward along the Ohio River. He stopped the car at a small park, took Lorene's hand and they strolled to a shaded wooden bench facing the river and the setting sun.

They sat, bodies touching, and Perry put his arm over her shoulder. She didn't push him away, and his arm tightened slightly into an impersonal hug. His touch radiated an affection that drew her like a magnet, and it eased the pain in her heart, but she refrained from turning to him to experience again the comfort of his strong embrace.

A cool breeze wafted from the river. Dark clouds hovered in the west, creating a sunset of vivid purple, red and yellow hues. They didn't speak for a long while, content to bask in closeness, overcome with memories. Words couldn't have expressed the comfort, the completeness, the rightness of the moment.

Sighing deeply, Perry brushed windblown strands of hair from Lorene's forehead. His fingers wended their way down the right side of her face as skillfully as a musician would tinkle the keys of a piano. He cupped her chin and slowly turned her face toward his.

"Do you remember the day we met?" he asked, his mouth curved with gentleness.

A hint of moisture lurked in Lorene's eyes and her intimate smile set his pulse racing. "You always could read my mind. I've been thinking about our first meeting all evening."

"I can still see you," he reminisced, "running out of the engineering building, with your book bag hanging open, scattering papers all over the steps."

"I was crying so hard I couldn't see, missed the last step and tumbled into your arms. You picked up my things, helped me to my car and invited me to join you for a sandwich. If I hadn't met you that day, I'd have dropped out of college. I'd just come from my adviser, who'd told me I wasn't going to make it in engineering school."

Perry pulled her into a closer embrace while she wrestled with that terrible blow to her ego. "I didn't know how I could possibly tell Dad. Since he didn't have a son, he'd insisted that I was the one to follow in his steps as an engineer. With your help, I did pass that semester, but by then I knew the adviser was right. Engineering wasn't for me."

"But you did great when you enrolled in a media-related curriculum. See where you are today!"

"I couldn't have done it without your help. You went home with me for moral support when I finally got the courage to tell my parents I'd changed my course of study. Just by being there, you kept Dad from bullying me into doing what he wanted."

"Your father blamed me for your change of plans, but I didn't mind. I'm happy I was there to help you. What are friends for, anyway?"

In the silence that followed, Lorene thought it might have been better if they'd continued as friends. But she couldn't be sorry for those weeks after she and Perry had known it was love rather than friendship that had created the infinite bond between them. His expression grew serious, his eyes wistful, and she wondered if he, too, remembered that evening when one intense kiss had suddenly changed their friendship to love.

It was the night before Easter break, and Perry had walked with her to the apartment. Her roommate had already left for the holidays, and Perry came inside with her. They'd often studied together in the apartment, but while she heated milk for hot chocolate, Perry roamed restlessly around the room picking up items and looking at them as if he hadn't seen them before.

He leaned against the table where they'd worked,

and their eyes met across the snack bar when she poured the steaming cups of chocolate. An undeniable magnetism flared between them, and as Perry's eyes searched her face and captured her eyes, for the first time she was conscious of Perry as a man. An electric spark couldn't have startled her more.

Their gazes held as he slowly circled the divider and reached hungry arms for her. His eagerness excited her and she cuddled into the circle of his arms. His mouth caressed hers, gentle as a raindrop, before she sensed the strength of his lips. When Perry released her, his black eyes brightened with pleasure.

"How long has this been here and we've overlooked it? How many weeks have we wasted being friends?"

Lorene had rested her head on his shoulder, knowing that they'd just taken a giant leap in their relationship. Even as she'd welcomed the change, she'd slowly mourned the days when they'd been best friends. If she recalled correctly, they never did drink the chocolate.

Pushing memories aside, Lorene wondered if they were embarking now on a third phase of their relationship. Was it possible to go from friends to lovers and back to friends again? After they'd experienced a satisfying, comfortable love, could they ever be content with anything less?

They returned to Riverview Ridge in silence, reliving the emotional toll the years of separation had brought. She invited him to come in, but he refused. He shook hands with her at the door, promising to contact her the next day. Lorene entered the apartment feeling strangely bereft. She consoled herself with the fact that he'd loved her once with all the vigor of youth. She was almost forty, and Perry was two years older, so was it reasonable to expect him to feel the same as he once had?

Still, when she lay down for the night, unbidden memories entered her mind as she recalled the contentment of being held against his strong body. That's all over, she told herself as she fluffed the pillows and tried to go to sleep. It's all over! You came here on business, and you'll have less to regret if you don't expect too much. Concentrate on your assigned duties, then cut your ties with Woodston and Perry Saunders.

Perry wasn't as indifferent to Lorene's physical allure as he seemed. He'd settled for a warm handshake when he'd wanted to gather her in his arms and bury his face in the soft curve of her shoulder. For more than a year they'd been inseparable, except on the few occasions when they'd gone to visit their parents. After twenty years it was inconceivable that he still remembered so much about Lorene.

Why hadn't she married? His tumultuous thoughts kept him awake most of the night.

In spite of her lack of sleep, Lorene awakened at six o'clock as usual. She pulled back the curtain beside her bed and peered out. Fog hovered over the river valley, and she decided to skip her usual morning run. She'd scout the area today to find a place where she could continue her daily exercise. Dottie could tell her if there was a trail from the house to the river.

The kitchen in the apartment was very small, but it was adequate for her needs. Breakfast was probably the only meal she'd eat here, but she'd have to buy a few groceries today. Dottie had provided an electric pot for heating water, tea bags, packages of decaffeinated coffee and sugar packets. While the water heated, Lorene unwrapped the two bran muffins she'd bought the day before and placed them in the small microwave.

While she ate, she flipped on the portable television conveniently placed on the kitchen counter. The news didn't pique her interest, and she hurried with her breakfast.

After showering, she dressed in shorts and a knit shirt and set up her laptop on a small desk in the bedroom. She checked the e-mail and answered a few messages that needed immediate attention. She picked up the file she'd gotten from Alma yesterday, but she was too restless to study it. The thought she'd been trying to stifle since she'd awakened finally thrust itself to the forefront of her mind.

Had she and Perry been given a second chance?

There was no use trying to follow her usual routine as if nothing had happened. As if the foundation of the secure life she'd spent years building hadn't trembled yesterday when Perry had suddenly reentered her life. It had taken years for her to get over Perry. Not that she'd ever forgotten him and the love they'd shared, but she had reached the place when she didn't think about him first thing when she opened her eyes in the morning. Sometimes several days could pass and she didn't wonder where he was, and dreams about him had become less and less frequent.

What would their lives be like today if she hadn't left Perry, or if she'd gone back to him and they'd married? Considering the wonderful man Perry had become, she believed he would have been a fine husband. If they'd gotten married, they could have had children now—children who would be starting college.

Lorene jumped when the phone rang. She leaned over and picked up the phone from the nightstand. Probably her parents checking on her, she thought, but it was Perry.

"Am I calling too early?" he asked.

"I've been up a long time. Remember, I'm a working woman—no sleeping in for me."

"Mr. Kincaid has scheduled the meeting for seven o'clock in the commission's office at the bank."

"How many people are on the commission?"

"A dozen or so—usually only five or six show up for the meetings."

"It's way too late for me to take on this promotion deal. We should have been working with the commission for at least a year."

Perry's laugh was deep and warm. Lorene envisioned his eyes crinkling from mirth and his lips curving with humor. She groaned inwardly, remembering the laughter they'd once shared together.

"Remember you're in small-town America now. Somebody comes up with a new idea every time we meet, and it was only two months ago that Mr. Kincaid decided to obtain professional promotion to put Woodston on the map. You can expect new ideas right up to the day of the celebration."

She feigned a groan. "I'll do the best I can, but I hope no one expects miracles."

"What are your plans for today? I have some free time this afternoon if you want me to show you around town."

Lorene hesitated. If she spent a lot of time with Perry, it would be more difficult for her when she left Woodston. She well remembered when she couldn't get enough of his company and wanted to be with him all the time, but wasn't she mature enough now to control her emotions? After all, she thought, I'm middle-aged! I certainly won't be carried away like I was before.

"I'll study the file Alma gave me this morning

and check out the town after lunch. It would be a big help if you came along.''

Perry had noticed her hesitation and understood her reluctance, for he felt the same way. If he saw her frequently—and how could they avoid it when they'd be associated so closely?—they might be tempted to revisit painful emotional paths. But in the long hours of the night, when he'd reviewed the past and contemplated the future, he'd made up his mind that he couldn't ask anything from Lorene except friendship.

''I'll pick you up around two o'clock.''

Lorene laid the phone aside wondering how she could concentrate on her work responsibilities if she saw Perry every day. But she hadn't become successful in the business world without exerting personal discipline, so she picked up the file folder and forced herself to read and study every plan the commission had in mind for Heritage Week—the culmination of Woodston's celebration the last week in September.

Lorene had learned quite a lot about Woodston from her reading, but as Perry drove through the business district, he gave a running commentary of the town's history.

''Woodston was founded two hundred years ago this month when western Kentucky was still a frontier. At first there wasn't anything except a fort and a few outlying farmsteads, but after steamboats revolutionized river transportation, the town became an important shipping center. The Native Americans, the Shawnees, in particular, moved westward and Woodston started to grow. After the Civil War, the economy plummeted for years, but during World War II the town took on new life.''

Lorene held a small tape recorder in her palm and she pushed the off button. ''You like it here, don't you?''

''Very much. My childhood was spent in small towns—we moved several times as a boy. Father was a preacher in Iowa, so big-city life isn't for me. I love working with the young people at college.'' He didn't add that association with the students eased his pain over the children he'd never had.

He drove out of town to Frontier Park, where a replica of a log fort was under construction. ''The park is located on the site of the original fort,'' he explained. ''During Heritage Week several people will come down the river on flatboats for the opening ceremonies to reenact life in the early 1800s. They'll live in the fort, wear period clothing and cook as the settlers did. Artisans will give daily demonstrations on making pioneer crafts.''

''Sounds like fun.''

''We want you to make all of this attractive to out-of-state groups, as well as snag the attention of schoolchildren in Kentucky and the adjoining states.''

''I'll make phone and computer contacts tomorrow and persuade some of our bus-company clients to arrange tours," Lorene answered, excitement stirring as it always did when she started a new project.

"The park covers thirty acres," Perry said. He pointed to a shaft on a high point above the river. "Except for that monument, very little has been done to develop the area. The fort will be permanent, available as a tourist attraction after the celebration is over."

"Is that path along the river suitable for running? I like to jog every day if possible, and I haven't seen any other likely place."

Perry's eyes lit up. "You're a runner? So am I."

"I noticed you're in good shape," Lorene said, willing her eyes not to sweep hungrily over his muscular physique.

"I spend a lot of time in the office, and if I'm not careful, I put on too much weight. I don't have opportunity for any other exercise, but I make time for running."

"Then it's safe for me to come out here alone."

"Yes. Many people use the park. But I run here several times a week. You can come when I do."

She lowered her eyes. "Don't tempt me, Perry."

"Why should it be a temptation?" He tilted her chin slightly, but hurriedly removed his hand as if the physical contact disturbed him. "We can't ignore what happened between us. Why can't we put it behind us and be friends? I'm happy you've entered my life again, and I want to see as much of you as possible.''

''That could be risky.''

''I'm determined that nothing will happen to cause any problem. And I know you feel the same way.''

He sounded so cheerful about their casual acquaintance that Lorene couldn't help asking in a husky whisper, ''Is it all over for you, Perry? Don't you feel anything at all?''

He placed his hands on her shoulders in a tender caress and his voice echoed her own longings. ''I'd thought, after reaching the mellow years, that my youthful yearnings were gone.'' His hands tightened possessively. ''But yesterday I learned I'd only fooled myself. You're as winsome and desirable as you were when you were nineteen. I made a promise to you once and I've never broken it. During the past twenty-four hours, other things I thought I'd forgotten have deleted all my preconceived ideas about what the future holds.''

''I haven't forgotten, either,'' she murmured.

Perry's eyes darkened and Lorene thought he was going to kiss her, but he released her and stepped back quickly.

''We'll have to forget what happened when we were in college and make the right choices this time. Since neither of us is married, there's no reason we can't be friends like we used to be.''

The flame in her heart ignited by Perry's love had

burned steadily for years, but his words almost extinguished it. She could never be satisfied with friendship. Maybe this meeting *had* been God-ordained. Perhaps God was trying to tell them it was time to stop pining for the past. If so, after her work was finished in Woodston, she'd go back to Pittsburgh, knowing at last that the break between them was final.

"Let's look over the fort and walk around my favorite running trail," Perry said. "It winds along the river for a mile and then curves through the trees back to the starting point. I'm going with some students to a seminar in Lexington tomorrow, but we can plan to run together on Monday morning."

She nodded, unable to talk. Perry had shifted gears from the past to the present too rapidly for her. But she obediently followed him into the fort, where workmen were putting the finishing touches on the blockhouse.

"I'll bring my camera tomorrow and get a few scenes to send out right away. My office staff will take care of distributing short clips to air on national programs. I'm getting excited about the celebration, and I've decided I want to stay for this project. I'm glad I didn't let my temper cause me to leave."

His eyes caressed her with a tender smile. "That makes two of us."

Lorene admitted Mr. Kincaid knew how to conduct a business meeting. At the outset, Perry stated that he and Lorene had been friends in college and were pleased to meet again after so many years. His explanation paved the way for them to be on a first-name basis. Perry introduced her to the other commission members and Lorene took particular note of two of them.

Zeb Denney, husband of Perry's secretary, was Woodston's chief of police. He was a quiet, broad-shouldered, short man.

The local historian, Reginald Peters, was in his eighties. A mop of gray hair hung untidily around his face, but his dark brown eyes were intelligent and alert. His ancestor had been one of Woodston's founding fathers, and while it was plain that Kincaid was in charge of the celebration, Peters's opinions also carried a lot of weight in the decision making.

Heritage Week would begin with a parade on the fourth Saturday in September. In addition to the reenactment at the fort, a steamboat replica, *River Queen,* would be on hand during the week to take people for rides up and down the Ohio, featuring a dinner cruise each evening. A carnival would be in town. Craft shows had been scheduled.

"Miss Harvey," Kincaid asked before the meeting adjourned, "do you have any questions?"

"As I understand, my job is to spread the news of the celebration nationwide. We can provide clips for all major television networks and numerous radio stations. But as far as I can determine, no financial arrangements have been made, leading me to the most important question—how much do you expect to spend for this publicity? Television advertising is expensive.''

All eyes turned toward Kincaid. He cleared his throat a time or two and riffled the pages on his desk. ''Perhaps you'd better come up with a proposal of what you recommend and how much it will cost.''

''Our representative should have done that and gotten your approval before we even moved on-site, but Mr. Cranston didn't do what he was supposed to do, so our agency, as well as Woodston, is suffering for it.''

''Can you estimate a price?'' Kincaid asked cautiously.

Believing it was a trifle late for caution, Lorene said, ''Not right now. But I'll work this weekend and have an estimate for you on Monday. If you can't afford us, I'll move out and there will be no charge to Woodston. To be honest, a smaller company would probably do as much for you as I will.''

Perry's heart plummeted. If the commission rejected the proposal, Lorene might leave in a few days.

He made it a point to ride down in the elevator with Lorene, and walked with her to the parking lot behind the bank. Zeb Denney and Reginald Peters sauntered along behind them, but when Perry opened the station wagon's door for Lorene, he said quietly, ''If Woodston can't afford your services and you go away next week, will you leave your telephone number and address?''

Her lips curved into a soft smile. ''You already have my telephone number. Circumstances are a lot different now than they were when I knew you before. When I leave Woodston, if it seems best for us to separate permanently, I'll tell you so. I've stopped running.'' She paused, and a pensive expression dimmed her eyes. ''Or at least, I think I have.''

The board members got into their cars and drove away. Perry's lips moved over hers, gently at first, then more insistent. After a few blissful moments she pushed on his chest to break the caress.

''Don't, Perry,'' she murmured. ''I can't handle this.''

''Sorry. I thought a kiss for old times' sake wouldn't hurt anything.''

Her hand was still on his chest, and she moved it to monitor his heartbeat, which was as rapid as hers.

''But you found out differently, didn't you?'' She moved away from him and slid into her vehicle. ''These next two months will go much more smoothly, Perry, if we maintain a strict business relationship. But if it turns out that we can't patch up our differences, I'll not make a mess of things like I did before. I won't disappear.''

As she drove away, Perry wondered how he'd feel if he knew she was leaving for the last time. But how could he offer her more than friendship? When he'd been at his lowest ebb, mentally and spiritually, he'd promised God that he would give up everything, including Lorene, for full-time Christian service. After he made that vow, warm peace had flooded his heart, and Perry believed he'd made the right choice. Now, remembering the touch of Lorene's lips, he wasn't so sure.

Chapter Four

Lorene spent Saturday morning walking along Woodston's streets to get a feel for the history of the town. The population was near five thousand, excluding college students, and except for a few small industries, most of the residents had jobs in Louisville and Evansville and commuted to work. Woodston College was the town's major employer.

Obviously, the glory days of the town had been the steamboat era. Lorene checked out renovated warehouses along Front Street, now housing numerous restaurants where any kind of food from sodas, ice cream, shakes, French fries, burgers and spaghetti to expensive steak cuts and shrimp was served. Small shops offered collectibles, crafts and souvenirs for sale.

The current Woodston business district was located on a high knoll safe from all except the most extreme floods. Front Street stores, however, had uneven floors and dark lines on buildings marking high-water stages when the Ohio River had flooded the town many times.

Lorene bought a burger and iced tea from a street vendor and sat on a concrete bench, looking out over the river, to enjoy her lunch. Several pleasure boats floated lazily back and forth, but they moved out of the way for a large towboat that moved upstream. There was something about the laid-back atmosphere of a small town that gave one a sense of security and well-being. Lorene could understand why Perry was satisfied here.

She spent an hour or more walking around the campus of Woodston Christian College, which was the focal point of the business district. The college had been founded before the Civil War, and the original building, Old Main, now housed the administrative staff, where Perry's office was located. Perry was gone for the day, and the campus seemed empty without him.

Many of the businesses along Main Street, in buildings that dated to the antebellum South, catered to the students. Woodston Banking and Trust, Mr. Kincaid's bank, was located in a three-story modern brick building, and Lorene went in to open a checking account for personal use during the time she was in Woodston.

In midafternoon she returned to Riverview Ridge, where Dottie and John were working in the yard.

Dottie waved her hand, and Lorene walked to the flower bed where Dottie was pulling weeds.

"We're trying to get the place in shape before Heritage Week," she said. "I'm booked up that week, so I'll be busy."

"I'm surprised I was able to get accommodations then," Lorene said.

"I'd just had a cancellation about an hour before you drove in," she said, "or I couldn't have taken you. Want to eat dinner with us this evening?"

"Yes, if it's not too late to make reservations. I've been looking over Woodston today for some ideas on planning the publicity. It's an interesting town."

"We think so, but we've only been here a few years. After John retired, we wanted a quieter place than Louisville, but still on the river. We heard that this property was for sale and decided it would be a good investment—a place for us to have a little income and give us a reason for getting out of bed in the morning."

"What time is dinner?"

"Six-thirty."

"I'll see you then. I've been grocery shopping, so I'd better put my cold things in the fridge, unpack the rest of my belongings and settle in for the long haul."

A carved mantel of oak, embellished with designs of oak leaves and pineapples, was centered in one wall of Riverview Ridge's dining room, with two original cupboards on each side. The cupboards were filled with antique dishes. A floral-patterned paper covered the walls above the wooden chair rail. The wide panels of the oak floor were highly polished, but numerous scars indicated the rough wear the wood had seen for over a century.

Several small tables were placed around the large room, providing seating capacity for twenty. Lorene joined a middle-aged couple from Illinois, who were traveling through Kentucky on a nostalgia journey retracing the places they'd visited during their honeymoon twenty-five years earlier. They showed Lorene pictures of their children and grandchildren. The meal was served family-style with a choice of country-fried chicken or baked fish, a variety of vegetables and salads and, for dessert, a fruit plate or rhubarb-raisin pie. The cuisine was evidently an attractive feature of Riverview Ridge.

Lorene and her companions spent over an hour at the table, and it was an enjoyable interlude, but when she excused herself and went to the apartment, Lorene stood for a long time staring out the window. Her eyes didn't focus on the pastoral setting, for she was in a wistful mood. While she'd been exerting all of her time and energy in building a successful business, Lorene hadn't often allowed herself to dwell on the things she was missing in life. Indeed, considering the unhappy marriages of her parents and her younger sister, Rose, she'd long ago concluded that she'd made the right decision to remain single. If marriage didn't offer any more love, understanding and companionship than her family's marriages demonstrated, she wasn't interested.

But visiting with the contented couple this evening had opened her eyes to the happiness and contentment possible in a marriage. The couple's life hadn't been without difficulties, but through sickness, disappointment and death, their love had expanded until it was warmer and stronger than it had been on their wedding day. The tender glances exchanged by husband and wife as they remembered their honeymoon had been Lorene's undoing. She was convinced that she and Perry could have had a similar marriage. Why hadn't she been strong enough to defy her parents and go back to Perry before it was too late?

Lorene leaned her head against the windowpane, but she didn't cry. Her anguish was too deep for tears. If the decision had been hers, after she'd gotten over her anger at Perry's rejection she would have found him again. But once she returned home and her parents learned about her affair with Perry, they took matters out of her hands. Her father had been transferred to another state, and she'd gone with her parents to enter another university. If she had it to do over, Lorene believed she would have defied them, but she hadn't been very assertive then, so she'd let Perry drift out of her life.

For months after their separation, Lorene had been angry at God for causing the rift between her and Perry, but when she got away from her parents she started going to church again. But one day she'd heard a sermon on the unpardonable sin that had puzzled and agitated her. She'd wondered since that time if she'd committed sins that couldn't be forgiven, but she was hesitant to bare her personal life to anyone. Who would have thought that an unexpected pregnancy could have caused so much heartache?

In spite of her doubts that God would forgive her, Lorene had continued to pray, and she believed God heard her at times, but other days there seemed to be a large gulf between her and Heaven that mere words couldn't bridge. Her spirits plummeted during those periods, and she feared her past would always stand in the way of complete communion with God. Perry knew most of her shortcomings. Perhaps she could talk with him about her spiritual doubts and questions. But on second thought, she decided Perry was the *last* person she should confide in.

Lorene was jolted out of her melancholy when Dottie called up the back stairs. "You're wanted on the phone."

Perry had her mobile phone number, so he wouldn't have called Riverview Ridge.

Lorene went to the head of the stairs. "Do you know who it is?"

"Alma Denney."

Lorene didn't hand out her cell phone number recklessly, but it would be all right for Perry's secretary to have it. And Dottie, too, should know if someone else tried to reach her through the B and B.

"Please give her my cell phone number and ask her to call me up here? Got a pencil to write it down?"

"Nope, but I've got a good memory."

Grinning, Lorene called off the telephone digits.

The interruption was welcome to Lorene. If she'd spent many more minutes thinking about what she'd missed with Perry, she would soon have indulged in a pity party, with herself as the only guest.

"Hello, Alma," Lorene said when her phone rang soon afterward. "What can I do for you?"

In the soft drawl that Lorene was beginning to recognize as the native dialect, Alma answered, "I called to invite you to church at the college chapel tomorrow morning. There won't be a large crowd, because many of the students go home on weekends, but our chaplain always has a good message. And we want you to have lunch at our house afterward. Perry usually has the noon meal with us on Sunday."

The invitation surprised Lorene, for she'd thought Alma resented her unexplained connection with Perry, and she hesitated. Was the woman seeking an opportunity to pry into her past? She had intended to go to church tomorrow, knowing that she could get some good ideas for publicity as she watched Woodston residents worship. And she wanted to see

Perry as much as she could while she was in Woodston. She must store up some new memories to cherish when she went back to Pittsburgh. The town had seemed empty today because he hadn't been here.

"Thank you. I'll be happy to come, although I can't stay late. I have to hand Mr. Kincaid a financial proposal Monday morning, and it isn't ready yet."

"Feel free to leave when you must," Alma assured her.

Alma waited for Lorene at the chapel door on Sunday morning, and they entered the small sanctuary to the sound of organ music. Zeb, Alma's husband, nodded a welcome to Lorene as she and Alma slid into a pew brightened by light through a stained-glass memorial window.

Lorene focused her thoughts on the minister's message, "The Unconditional Love of God," based on the Scripture passage from Jeremiah 31. "I have loved you with an everlasting love; I have drawn you with loving kindness."

"God's love is not fickle like the devotion of humans," the minister stressed at the outset of his sermon, "which is often motivated by the actions of those we love.

"His love is unconditional. He loves us if we're good. He loves us if we're bad. God doesn't treat His children as some earthly father might, saying to His child, 'If you'll be good, I'll love you.' There is absolutely nothing we can do that can make God love us more or less than He does right now. Even when our actions grieve the heart of God, His love remains steadfast.''

If these words were true, God had forgiven the sins of her youth. Had she worried needlessly about the one thing she'd done that she thought God, and Perry, could never forgive? Maybe it *was* God's plan for Kenneth Cranston to leave her employ so she'd be forced to come to Woodston and set things right with Perry. She blinked and picked up the thread of the message.

''Many people live in fear that the revelation of some skeleton in the closet will ruin their reputation. That isn't necessary for those who've trusted Christ. Mistakes and sorrows are common to everyone, including Christians, but the Scriptures promise that God's forgiving love remains steadfast.''

Lorene's face flushed, and she felt faint when the minister summed up his sermon. ''Turn your attention to the Biblical account of Jesus's confrontation with a woman who had committed adultery, an unforgivable sin in ancient times, one punishable by death. Jesus dealt first with the woman's accusers, reminding them of their own shortcomings. They dropped the charges. He knew the woman was guilty of the sin, but He spoke kindly to her. 'I don't condemn you. Go now and leave your life of sin.' That incident confirms Jesus's unconditional love.''

Lorene squirmed uncomfortably, thankful when

the minister closed his sermon and gave the benediction.

She hadn't seen Perry, but when he joined her and the Denneys in the foyer, she assumed he'd been sitting behind them.

"I've invited Lorene to join us for lunch, Perry," Alma explained. "We're having a cookout."

"Alma's barbecues are famous," Perry said. "You'll be glad you came."

"How do I find your home?" Lorene asked Alma.

"It's a little difficult to explain, so why don't you follow Zeb and me?" Alma said. "Or you could leave your car here and drive out with Perry."

"Why don't you do that, Lorene?" Perry's invitation seemed genuine, not one that was forced on him by Alma's suggestion. First Mr. Kincaid, and now Alma throwing them together.

"Give me time to get a pair of sandals out of the station wagon. I don't want to spend the day in heels. Back in a minute."

Excited to be spending some leisure time with Perry, Lorene hurriedly changed shoes and walked back to his car. As she buckled her seat belt, she asked, a humorous lilt in her voice, "Is Alma matchmaking?"

Perry chuckled. "Could be. She's been trying to get me married ever since I moved here, although that may not be the case today—she's always free with her luncheon invitations."

"If she only knew!"

"Don't underestimate her," Perry warned. "She's pretty shrewd."

"That sermon hit home this morning, as you must know it would. Sounds as if the minister knew I was coming."

Perry slanted a look in her direction, and his eyebrows rose in surprise.

"Surely you aren't still concerned over what happened years ago? We confessed our wrongdoing to God, and He forgave us. I don't doubt that in the least."

But Perry's eyes shifted away from her as a confusing thought surfaced. Was she referring to the one time they'd strayed? Or had she continued a promiscuous lifestyle? Lorene hadn't been far from his thoughts since she'd entered his life again, and although he was physically and emotionally drawn to her, he wasn't sure he could ever trust her again. If she'd disappeared from his life once without warning, would she do the same thing again? He must go slowly in reviving a relationship with Lorene. It was unthinkable to deliberately invite the trauma he'd experienced when she'd abandoned him before.

Lorene missed his perplexed, uneasy glance as she stared straight ahead, wondering if God had meant the sermon for her. Could she accept the principle of God's unconditional love in relation to her past? She'd have to think of that later. Today she wanted to enjoy Perry's company—she might not have many more opportunities.

The Denneys lived in a modest home on the western edge of town. Their backyard sloped gently toward the Ohio River. Zeb manned the grill on the patio, and he was busily coating beef ribs with barbecue sauce when Lorene and Perry arrived. Perry left his coat and tie in the car, making Lorene wish she could have gone to the apartment and changed into casual clothes.

Perry stretched out in a lounge chair and breathed deeply. He was always bushed after a heavily scheduled week, and he usually sneaked a nap while Zeb and Alma prepared the meal, but he didn't intend to sleep today and miss any of Lorene's company.

Alma came out of the house with a tray of utensils, and Lorene asked, "What can I do to help?"

"I have vegetables and salads to carry out, but let's wait fifteen minutes or so until the ribs are well-done. Want to walk down to the river?"

"You have a great view," Lorene commented as they sauntered toward the Ohio. Speedboats and motorboats, towing water-skiers, riffled the waters of the Ohio, which splashed against the stone retaining wall.

"We live here because of the scenery, but this land is lower than the town site, and when the river floods and the water inches closer and closer to our house, it's not so pleasant. We have flood scares two or three times a year, and our home has been flooded twice during the ten years we've lived here.''

"Pittsburgh has its share of high water, too.''

"Have you always lived in Pittsburgh?''

"No. I worked in several cities before I decided to find a permanent home. My parents live in Pennsylvania, and I feel duty bound to be close to them if they should need any help.''

"You knew Perry before you moved to Pittsburgh, then,'' Alma stated with a watchful eye on Lorene's face.

"A long time before that,'' Lorene said. Without a flicker of the eye or, hopefully, any other telltale signs, she continued, "Perry and I were friends in college until I left at the end of my junior year to finish my education at another university. We didn't keep in touch, so it was quite a surprise to see him again after so many years. But a pleasant surprise.''

"Hey, Alma,'' Zeb shouted. "These ribs are about done.''

Alma turned toward the house, and Lorene escaped further questioning for the time being. Perry was asleep in the lounge chair, and Alma tiptoed past him.

"He likes to take a nap on Sunday afternoon,'' she said quietly, shaking her head. "If I didn't look after him, he'd never get any rest.'' She smiled apologetically. "That's the reason I was hesitant the other day when you came to the office. I figured you were a salesperson.''

Lorene laughed. "I guess I am at that, but I was irked to be put on hold at so many places in one day. I work long hours, too, and I don't like people to waste my time. I was also annoyed because I had to give up my summer vacation with my family to come to Woodston."

"That's too bad," Alma sympathized.

"It still rankles a little, but this town is rather laid-back compared to what I'm used to, so the slower pace is a vacation from my usual routine."

"You'll miss seeing your family, though," Alma suggested as she handed Lorene a platter of roasted corn on the cob.

Lorene smiled wryly. "Oh, I don't know," she said. "I try to be a dutiful daughter, and Mother makes a big deal of our vacationing together, so I feel a responsibility to comply." Taking a deep breath, she added, "But my parents have a tendency to treat me as if I'm still a teenager, and that annoys me. Rose, my younger sister, usually brings her two unruly children, so by the end of two weeks I'm always relieved to go back to work."

When Lorene placed the platter on the picnic table, Perry stretched and sat up, still sleepy eyed, and she turned away with a sudden pang in her heart. She'd forgotten how vulnerable he looked when he first awakened and sleep had softened the glint of his dark eyes.

"Sorry," he said. "I didn't intend to go to sleep."

"We must be boring company," Zeb said, chuckling.

"Perry needs to rest when he can," Alma retorted. "Mr. Kincaid is always piling too much work on him. Besides," she added with a knowing look at her husband, "he's not the only man I know who naps on Sunday afternoon."

Zeb winked at Lorene. "Alma only had one chick of her own to mother, so she took Perry under her wing."

"And I appreciate it, too," Perry said. "I'd probably never remember to eat if Alma didn't put food before me."

"Yeah," Zeb answered. "You need a wife to look after you, boy."

"Seems I've heard that mentioned before," Perry said laughingly, "but right now I'm too interested in a plate of ribs to dwell on serious things."

The Denneys were amiable hosts, and Lorene enjoyed the afternoon with them. They made her feel like an honored guest, and she figured that was why people coveted invitations to their barbecues, but the food was excellent, too. She learned quite a lot about their area and the upcoming celebration, taking mental notes to help in planning the publicity for Woodston.

They lingered over apple pie and coffee until shortly after three o'clock, when Perry said, "I've got a board meeting at four. Ready, Lorene?"

"Yes. I have a busy evening facing me, too. I need to finish that proposal for Mr. Kincaid."

She thanked Alma for the invitation and Zeb for preparing the tasty meat and received their sincere invitation to visit them any time. Being with the Denneys had given Lorene a new insight into marriage. Even their playful bickering demonstrated the Denneys' mutual affection. Lorene's parents never seemed to have any fun together. Would it have been different with her and Perry?

It wasn't likely she would ever know, but the more she was around Perry, the more she found herself succumbing to his virility, remembering all the things that had first attracted her to him—the tenderness of his touch, his sensitivity to her every need and his air of cheerful expectation. She'd never met another person who exemplified all the characteristics she desired in a man, and she intended to see him as much as possible in the next few weeks.

Reaching the campus parking lot, Perry said, "Do you want to run with me tomorrow morning? I usually leave the house at seven o'clock."

"Yes, I'd like that. Should I meet you at the park?"

"I'll come by Riverview Ridge for you about seven o'clock."

"By the way, where do you live, Perry?"

"I have a cottage on the campus. It's only three rooms, but big enough for me." Perry walked around the car to open the door and handed her a business card. "You should have my home telephone number and e-mail address if you need to reach me."

She took the card. As she looked up at him, all her past loneliness and frustration joined in an upsurge of yearning, and her eyes darkened as she held his gaze. Perhaps sensing her confusion and anxiety, he reached for her hand and lifted it to his lips.

"Seeing you again has given me a new lease on life," Perry said. "I've been annoyed with Mr. Kincaid for pushing the responsibility of this celebration on me, but now I'm happy that he did. This has been the most enjoyable day I've had for a long time."

Lorene's heart reacted violently to the significance of his words, but she couldn't speak past the lump in her throat. She walked wordlessly to her car, tormented by confusing emotions.

Chapter Five

With no idea how much money the commission expected to spend on PR, Lorene worked for hours trying to come up with a proposal for Mr. Kincaid. She wanted to make her offer inviting enough that the commission would accept it, but not so low that her company would lose money on the project. To make the proposal more attractive, she decided to forgo her personal commission, something she had never done before.

Slightly disgusted at herself, she knew why she was so interested in representing Woodston. She was grasping at straws—just any excuse to be around Perry, even if it did cost her money. But she'd found out long ago that there were things more important than money. If she had it to do over again, when her parents had threatened to cut off her tuition money if she married Perry, she'd have defied them.

Up until that time she'd never had a job, for her parents had insisted that they pay for her education so she could devote herself to studying. She'd realized later that was just another way of controlling her. And since Perry had barely made enough to pay his own expenses, it had seemed impossible for them to marry until after they finished college.

More than once, Lorene's hands stilled on the computer as she reflected upon the odd, almost miraculous turn of events that had brought her and Perry together after so many years. Was it really true, as Perry said, that it was God's will for them to meet again? If so, why?

Of all the media consultants in the country, why would Mr. Kincaid choose her company to represent Woodston? According to Alma, he'd gotten a list of consultants off the Internet, had checked out their Web sites and settled on Lorene's firm without contacting any other. And Kenneth Cranston had been dissatisfied for several months. Why had he chosen this particular time to resign—a time when all her other employees were occupied and no one but Lorene was available to take the assignment?

Many people would term their meeting as Lady Luck, happenstance or destiny. But she thought Perry might be right—that God did have a purpose in reuniting them. Lorene hadn't been faithful in her spiritual worship over the past several years, but she hadn't forgotten the biblical truths she'd learned soon after she'd become a Christian.

Her parents were church members, but they'd seldom attended worship services, and the teachings of the Bible made no difference in the way they lived. When she'd met Perry, he'd invited her to attend Christian meetings with him. After a few months, she'd accepted Jesus Christ as her personal Savior, and her life had taken on new meaning as she studied the Scriptures, especially Jesus's Sermon on the Mount, which had given her direction on how to live a meaningful life.

She left the computer and wandered into the living room. She picked up a Bible from the antique walnut lamp stand and searched for a verse she'd once committed to memory.

"When I was woven together in the depths of the earth, Your eyes saw my unformed body. All the days ordained for me were written in Your book before one of them came to be."

As she understood that verse, even before a child was born, God had a plan for its life, but He didn't create people to be robots. Each individual had the opportunity to make decisions about life. And if people made the wrong choices, did God give up on them, or did He give them a second chance?

Abraham and Sarah had made a questionable choice when they'd taken matters into their own hands to provide an heir when they had a concubine give birth to a son. But in God's own time, Isaac, the child God had promised them, was born. In spite of the lack of faith exhibited by Sarah and Abraham,

God kept His promise. So if God forgave their impetuosity, surely He had forgiven Perry and Lorene for their youthful indiscretion.

Jonah was given a second chance after he turned in the opposite direction when God told him to take the message of salvation to Nineveh.

Peter, disciple of Jesus, had denied his Lord, but Jesus forgave him and Peter became an important leader in the early Church.

Lorene knew she'd made many poor choices, and she'd made a terrible mistake in not trusting Perry. She should have known he wouldn't have deserted her. She could think of many reasons to justify her response to his apparent desertion, but why bother? The past was behind them. Now they had to decide how to deal with the present opportunity.

The only changes she could note in Perry had been for the better, and if Perry's attentiveness was any indication, he wasn't opposed to resuming their relationship. But their lives had taken such diverse turns, she didn't see how they could ever make a life together.

Perry was happy in small towns. Lorene needed to live in a metropolitan area to continue her work. While Lorene didn't let her parents dictate to her anymore, she tried to avoid dissension in her family. She could imagine the furor if her father learned that Perry had come back into her life. And she could never understand why her father hadn't approved of Perry. She suspected that he wouldn't have liked anyone she wanted to marry, for her sister's husband hadn't suited him, either. In spite of her protestations to the contrary, her parents had blamed Perry for everything that had happened. But she'd listened to her parents once and lived to regret it, so she wouldn't let them stand in the way of any future happiness she could find with Perry.

A heavy layer of fog hung over the river when they arrived at Frontier Park, and the grass was slippery with dew.

Looking at the sky, Perry said, "Going to be hot today. That's the reason I like to run early in the morning. During the winter I wait until midday."

"At home I run in late evening. There are several quiet streets close to my apartment where I can jog, as well as a few nearby parks."

They limbered up with five minutes of exercises, and Perry said, a smile creasing his face, "You set the pace, and if you're too fast for me, I'll let you know."

"Is the trail wide enough for us to run side by side?"

"In places. Take off, and if the two-mile run isn't enough, we can go around twice."

"Once is enough for today."

She started out at a fast walk, then broke into gentle jogging steps. Following her, observing the natural grace of her body and considering the time they'd missed being together, Perry was overcome by a terrible sense of bitterness and loss. Lost years, when having Lorene by his side would have enriched his life with the happiness of fathering children and having a family life. If God was giving them a second chance, he wanted to take advantage of the opportunity. But he must be sure that he wasn't mistaking his own physical and emotional needs for what God wanted him to do.

Lorene flashed a smile at him when he reached her side. They passed an elderly couple strolling along the trail, and they jogged to one side when three teenagers whizzed by them.

"Members of the high school's track team," Perry explained. "I can't keep up with them."

The parking lot was full of cars when they finished their run, and several construction workers had arrived to continue work at the fort. Lorene realized that she and Perry must meet only in the public's eye to avoid any act-first-and-think-later behavior. With several people in sight, it seemed like a safe place to talk.

"Let's sit at a picnic table for a few minutes to cool down," she suggested. Perry took two bottles of water from his car and they sipped on them as she chose a table far enough away from the fort so their conversation couldn't be overheard.

"I have a proposal ready for Mr. Kincaid, and as soon as I shower and change clothes, I'll deliver it to his office."

"Should I ask how much it's going to cost Woodston?" Perry said with a sly grin.

"I made up two proposals. Even if the commission wants nothing more than contacts with radio stations and newspapers, the cost will exceed $20,000. But if Mr. Kincaid is intent on having national television coverage, he's going to have to dig deeper than that—a lot deeper. I've given him a fluctuating cost, depending upon how much he wants me to do. Does Woodston have that kind of money?"

He gestured slightly with his right hand. "Not in the treasury, but both Kincaid and Reginald Peters are rich, and they take up the slack when we have a shortfall."

She took a deep breath and wouldn't make eye contact with him. "While the commission makes a decision, I've decided to fly to Atlantic City and join my family for a few days. Then I'll go to Pittsburgh for at least a week's work in the office. If my proposal is accepted, I can do the preliminary work in Pittsburgh as well, or probably better, than I can in Woodston."

"If they turn down your proposal, you won't be back?"

"I'm not running away, Perry."

"I'll take you to the airport."

It was tempting, but she said, "No, thanks. I've arranged to fly from the Louisville airport. I'll drive and leave my station wagon in the parking lot."

He was quiet as they returned to Woodston. When Perry stopped in front of her apartment, he laid his hand on her left shoulder. "Why? Why are you going?" His eyes searched her face as he tried to read her thoughts.

After a few minutes of uneasy silence she said, "Things are moving too fast for me. We can't bridge a gulf of twenty-plus years in a few days, not even in a few months. We've both changed—we should have put the recklessness of youth behind us by now, but I'm not sure we have. I need some time away from you."

His grip tightened on her shoulder, his dark eyes never leaving her face for a moment. "You may be right, but answer me one thing—do you *want* to try again?"

Just his touch on her shoulder sent waves of pleasurable sensation through her body, and it was hard for Lorene to keep her thoughts focused. Her mind took off in flighty jaunts of ecstasy, making it difficult to order her confused emotions. Was now the time to unburden all her guilt feelings? How honest could she be with him? Out of her turbulent thoughts she sorted one certainty—she didn't want to lose him this time.

She looked at him quickly, fondly. "Yes, Perry, I do."

His arm slid down her arm and tightened around the tense fingers that lay in her lap. She relaxed under his soft, warm touch, and he lifted her hand to his lips.

"Thanks for being honest with me. We'll work it out some way—I don't know how, but it'll be all right." He opened the door for her. "I won't call you, but you know how to reach me if you want to talk."

Two weeks later when Lorene started her return to Woodston, she had more concerns than she'd had when she left. While spending five days with her family, Lorene checked in at the office daily and learned from Opal, her office manager, that Mr. Kincaid had contacted the office. She returned his call, and he reported that the commission had opted for the more expensive plan, with the stipulation that she make a report to the commission on her progress and cost each week, so they might ask her to decrease the publicity if necessary.

During the next week she'd coordinated her plans with Opal, who would handle most details from the office while Lorene stayed in Woodston. The last week in August she intended to interview Gaston Kincaid, Reginald Peters, Zeb Denney and Perry for national appearances. And since Dottie was such a colorful character, she thought she might use her in some way, too. She'd secured the cooperation of a network early-morning show—one of their representatives would spend several days in Woodston during Heritage Week and broadcast daily scenes featuring the celebration. She'd also gotten several bookings from tour bus companies.

Lorene had no worries about her publicity plans. But she was disturbed about her parents' interest in the celebration, and their hint that they might come to Woodston for a few days. Lorene's ancestors had lived in Kentucky, and her father had developed a recent interest in tracing his roots. Lorene did all she could to discourage them without arousing suspicion, for she knew her parents *must not* find out that Perry lived in Woodston.

She'd refrained from calling Perry, but she was disappointed that he hadn't called her. The night before she caught a plane back to Kentucky, she telephoned his home. Lorene felt like screaming when his answering machine picked up, but she swallowed her disappointment and said, "This is Lorene. My plane arrives in Louisville tomorrow, early afternoon. I should be back in Woodston by evening."

The words *I've missed you* hovered on her tongue, and she quickly hung up before she could say them. She stayed up until midnight hoping he'd return her call, but he didn't.

Her flight from Pittsburgh was delayed an hour, and it was after four o'clock before she landed, picked up the station wagon and started for Woodston on Interstate 64 through Indiana. Fifty miles from Evansville, her cell phone rang. She pulled to the side of the road and answered.

"Hello," Perry said, "I hoped I could reach you."

She hadn't been this excited over Perry when she was a sophomore in college. A matron now, she should have more control over her emotions.

"Everything all right in Woodston?"

"It will be when you get here. I've been counting the days until you returned. I hoped you'd telephone, and then when you called last night I was gone." She sensed the disappointment in his voice.

"I didn't want anything in particular—I just thought someone on the commission should know I'd be back today. My work in Pittsburgh is organized now so I can stay in Woodston until the celebration is over. Opal, the office manager, can handle everything until then."

"Where are you now?"

"North of Evansville, so it shouldn't be much longer."

"I'll come meet you, and we can have dinner together."

"That sounds good to me. Let's meet at the same restaurant where we ate a couple of weeks ago. My treat this time!"

"I'll take you up on that," he said, and the laughter in his voice was infectious. "See you soon."

Before she drove on, Lorene dropped her head to the steering wheel. *God, how can I be so happy and so miserable at the same time? What's in the future for us? I can't bear to live without him, now that*

I've found him again. But I've got a lot on my conscience.

Lorene drove into a rest stop to freshen up her makeup, went on to the restaurant, found a bench in the shade and waited forty-five minutes before Perry arrived. He parked his car beside her station wagon, hurried toward her, put an arm around her shoulders and gave her an affectionate hug.

"I was never really sure I'd ever see you again until this minute."

"Don't you trust me yet? I told you I'd be back. I didn't tell you that when I left you before."

"I know, but I've missed you. We're together now. Nothing else matters. Are you hungry?" he asked as, with his arm still around her shoulders, they walked into the restaurant.

"I'll say! We didn't have anything except snacks on the plane, and I didn't stop to eat after I got to Louisville."

All she'd wanted to do when she deplaned was to head for Woodston as rapidly as possible. Being away from Perry for only two weeks had caused Lorene to recall vividly the other time they'd separated, when she'd had to learn to live without him.

After they'd ordered, Perry asked, "Mr. Kincaid is beside himself anticipating all the things you've got lined up for us. The celebration starts in four weeks, and I hope we're ready. If he'd stop coming up with new ideas, we'd be all right."

Her eyebrows arched inquisitively. "Surely he

hasn't come up with something new at this late date!''

"Oh, yes! He has a bee in his bonnet to invite Jon Preston to make an appearance. He'll be after you about that as soon as he knows you're in Woodston.''

"Who's Jon Preston?''

"I had to ask, too,'' he said with a grin. "He's an up-and-coming Nashville recording artist who's become an overnight sensation. He's been appearing in Branson, Missouri, all summer. Mr. Kincaid wants to book him for our celebration before Preston returns to Nashville for recording sessions and appearances at the Grand Ole Opry.''

"I don't know anything about Preston, but I've booked other celebrities. Woodston will have to put down a *lot* of money to get him. And musicians that important have to be booked months ahead, so it isn't likely he'll be free to come to Woodston on such short notice.''

"Mr. Kincaid's granddaughter is a Preston fan, and she's been pestering him to invite the music star.''

"Sounds as if I'm going to be earning my money, and then some, until Heritage Week is history,'' Lorene said.

"And then what?'' Perry asked. "What happens to us after that?''

"If I do all the things I've committed to do for Woodston, I won't have any time to worry about us.

When I'm involved in a promotion, that's all I can think about.''

His hand was lying on the table, and she covered it with hers.

"We'll need to have a long talk, Perry. There are several things I have to say to you, and your reaction to what I say will determine our future. But right now I must give my full attention to Woodston for the next month.''

Lorene was obsessed with the idea that if her parents came to Woodston, she had to level with Perry before then, but when was the right time? Certainly not in this restaurant.

Perry observed her somber face, and he wondered what had happened to Lorene in the years they'd been separated that would affect their future relationship. "I can live with that,'' he agreed. "Tell me what I can do to make your work easier.''

"I need moral support more than anything else, I suppose, because my plans are complete and most of the appointments are confirmed. I'll have photographers in town next week to tape an interview with several of you who're involved in the celebration. Clips of the program will be used for spotlight advertising on the major networks and their member stations in this area.''

"That will be exciting for local residents.''

"Representatives of several TV channels will be in Woodston during the week of celebration. Short spots about Woodston's history and bicentennial plans will be aired on cable stations in many states north of the Ohio River and east of the Mississippi.''

Perry's eyes gleamed with admiration as he looked at her. ''You're good at your job. I'm happy you found a vocation that pleased you.''

Her voice was rich with laughter. ''And I'm glad I realized I wasn't cut out to be an engineer, and that you helped me talk my parents out of the idea. It was hard for Dad to give up the conviction that because he was an engineer, I ought to be one, too.'' She looked at Perry keenly. ''Both of us spent a lot of difficult days in engineering classes not to have continued in the profession. I couldn't make the grades, but you didn't have any problem. Seems a shame that you aren't using what you studied.''

''Sometimes I've wished God had called me into full-time Christian service before I started engineering school, but the degree opened a lot of doors when I worked to pay my way through the seminary. So all that studying and work wasn't wasted.''

''And if we both hadn't been enrolled in engineering school, we might not have met.''

''That's true,'' Perry agreed, ''but I believe in my heart that God meant us to be together. Just because we messed up along the way doesn't mean that His will won't eventually be realized in our lives. I'm praying that some way, somehow it will.''

Chapter Six

Lorene spent the rest of the week working with photographers and planning for the interview, which was taped on Friday in the completed fort. Reginald Peters, a colorful character, dressed in a dark gray suit and matching wide-brimmed hat, was introduced as a Kentucky Colonel. For the benefit of the viewing audience, Peters explained that the Honorable order of Kentucky Colonels had been founded in 1932, and later incorporated as a charitable organization. The order included not only Kentuckians but men and women—government leaders, business persons and entertainers—from other countries. Only a sitting governor of The Commonwealth of Kentucky could appoint a Kentucky Colonel, Peters said. Peters spoke slowly, and fondly, of his family.

"My ancestor came to Kentucky with George Rogers Clark during his campaign to drive the British out of the Northwest Territory during the War for Independence. He liked the country, so he stayed behind, living in the wilderness until the war was over. Then he settled on the land where Woodston is located today and sent word back east urging his former neighbors to join him. Although the Indian threat was all but over in Kentucky, the settlers built Fort Woodston for protection in an emergency, but to my knowledge, they never had to take refuge in it. The little village that grew up around the fort expanded into a city with the coming of the steamboat in the early part of the nineteenth century.''

Gaston Kincaid tended to be wordy as he explained the present-day benefits of Woodston, and Lorene flagged some of his comments to delete in the final editing of the film.

Perry spoke of the history of Woodston Christian College. ''The college was organized by northern missionaries who came to the region soon after the War Between the States. Kentucky had remained in the Union during the war, but many residents in the county had fought with the Confederacy, and wounds were still too fresh to allow spiritual unity. The missionaries believed that education would be a factor in healing the wounds between the two sections. From a handful of students, the college has grown to a student body of over five thousand.''

Dottie, with her flamboyant personality, outlined Woodston's Heritage Week. ''There's something for everybody, folks! What's your pleasure? Come run in the minimarathon that winds through five miles of our rural county. Bring your crafts and talents and display them in new Fort Woodston. Clog to the beat of some of the best bluegrass bands in the nation. Eat hot dogs and hand-cranked ice cream while listening to music by top entertainers. It's here for you, folks. Woodston, Kentucky—the last week in September. These celebrations happen only once in a century. You won't want to miss this one.''

When the clips of the panel presentation were presented on the local cable station, Lorene was pleased with the coverage. Her staff in Pittsburgh reported good feedback on their ads, and she knew the campaign had been effective when people from as far away as Florida telephoned for reservations in the local motels. By the first week of September, all the motels were booked solid for Heritage Week, and half the reservations had been made by out-of-state residents. Woodston's Chamber of Commerce started referring travelers to Evansville for lodging.

While all her other plans were jelling, Lorene was finding it difficult to get a commitment from Jon Preston's staff, and she often complained to Perry about Mr. Kincaid's haphazard methods. Perry offered a sympathetic ear and calmed her nerves when the pace became too hectic.

Lorene had been awake for over an hour when the phone rang, but she hadn't gotten out of bed. Incessant rain on the roof and eaves dripping outside her window discouraged the half-mile walk to the river that she took on the mornings she didn't run with Perry. Usually she liked a walk in the rain, but not today, when she was down in the dumps anyway.

She didn't want to speak to anyone, either, but on the fourth ring she languidly stretched a hand from under the covers and pushed the talk button on the telephone. The caller did nothing to lighten her mood.

"It's your fortieth birthday! Best wishes."

As if she needed a reminder!

"Thanks for letting me know, Mother."

"To think my firstborn is forty years old today! Where has the time flown?" Celeste Harvey continued her monologue on the past, apparently unaware that she was pushing Lorene's irritable buttons.

When Lorene didn't respond, Celeste said, "You aren't upset about turning forty, are you?"

"I can think of days I've anticipated more than this one."

"Oh, forty isn't so bad, but I thought I'd die when I reached fifty. A half-century old seemed intolerable."

"Then I have that to look forward to, I guess."

"We sent you a card and a check, but it may be late. Are you going to do anything special for the big day?"

Shaking herself mentally, Lorene knew she had to stop acting like a spoiled kid. She sat up in bed and answered in a pleasant voice, "Not really. No one here knows it's my birthday, so it will be just another workday as far as I'm concerned. Thanks for calling, though—it's nice to be remembered. How's Dad?"

"Just fine, and Rose is, too. The kids are back in school, and she's driving them back and forth each day, so she doesn't have much free time."

Celeste talked for twenty minutes and she didn't mention the celebration, so Lorene's mind was at ease when her mother said goodbye. Apparently they'd decided not to come to Kentucky. They couldn't have given her a better birthday gift.

Lorene didn't know why she was so melancholy about reaching forty, but it had been tugging at her mind all week. One of her co-workers had turned forty a few years ago, and her husband had thrown a party for his wife—an over-the-hill party, he'd called it. All the decorations, even the cake icing, were black. Everyone had seemingly had a hilarious time—except Lorene, who'd started wondering at what point one reached the zenith of life. Since that time, she'd dreaded her fortieth birthday.

She wished she had someone to talk to about her hang-ups on the subject, but it might be better that no one in Woodston knew. That way, she could ignore the milestone she'd just reached. She'd thought of mentioning it to Alma or Dottie, who'd passed their fortieth birthdays many years before and had survived. But if she told anyone, it might get back to Perry.

They'd celebrated her twentieth birthday together—had made quite an occasion of it, as least as much of an occasion as they could afford. Knowing that her favorite flower was the yellow rose, Perry had stretched his budget and bought her a single rosebud corsage. Then they'd taken a bus into the city for dinner. She'd worn a beige dress, a birthday gift from her parents, that complemented the corsage.

The details of that day were etched in her memory, including the taxi ride from the bus station to a ritzy hotel restaurant. It had been raining that day, too, and the doorman had come out with a large umbrella to escort her into the lounge. To a background of music by a stringed-instrument trio, they'd dined on shrimp cocktail, stuffed flank steak, mashed potatoes, Oriental mixed vegetables, cabbage-and-pepper slaw and warm banana bread. Perry had even arranged for the kitchen staff to serve a small chocolate cake while the musicians played "Happy Birthday." Memories of the simple observance, which had shot Perry's budget to pieces, were more precious to Lorene than any elaborate birthday party her parents had planned when she was a child. On every anniversary of her birth since then, she'd remembered her twentieth birthday as a special occasion, because she'd celebrated it with Perry.

She was still in bed when the phone rang again,

but she answered this time with more alacrity. At the sound of Perry's voice, the sun broke through the clouds, spreading beams of light across the hardwood floor, and her heart's burden eased, as well.

"How are you this rainy morning?" he asked cheerfully.

"Lazy," she said. "I haven't gotten out of bed."

"I'm free this afternoon and evening. Let's have dinner together. I could do with a break, and you probably need to get away from Woodston's heritage for a few hours."

Had he remembered her birthday? Was this the reason for his invitation? Could he have remembered after twenty years?

"I'd love to go. What time?"

"Let's leave about midafternoon. There's a restaurant near Louisville that I think you'll like. I'm not sure what time I'll get away, so I'll come to the apartment for you. I'm sure Dottie won't mind if a gentleman comes to your door."

With a light laugh she said, "No, she hasn't placed any restrictions on me."

She said goodbye and cradled the phone receiver softly. Her low spirits disappeared as if they'd never been. Jumping out of bed, she performed a Highland fling around the room that would have made her Scot ancestors proud. Pretty good footwork for a woman of forty!

Knowing that she would spend the evening with Perry was the only catalyst Lorene needed to start her day's work. She had a lot of correspondence to handle, but first she was inspired to worship God.

She brewed a cup of coffee and took it to the small balcony that had steps leading to the backyard. Lorene sat on the top step and looked toward the river, sniffing the moist air appreciatively. The landscape seemed refreshed after the night's rain. She remembered a Bible verse she'd learned in college chapel, "If we confess our sins, He is faithful and just to forgive our sins, and to cleanse us from all unrighteousness."

As Lorene observed the cleansed landscape, she asked God to purify her own soul. *God, have I committed an unpardonable sin that You can never forgive? Or are You unable to see the sin through the blood of Jesus that brought cleansing to my soul? I believe that's true, God, but sometimes I still have doubts. When I'm completely sure of Your forgiveness, I'll go to Perry and unburden the weight of my sin and ask his forgiveness, too.*

Lorene whizzed through her morning's work, answering e-mails and telephoning Pittsburgh to check how many buses would be coming to Woodston during Heritage Week. She made a few calls to see if local restaurants would set up refreshment stands on Front and Main Streets, because if large crowds came, the restaurants wouldn't have enough seating. At noon she ate a carton of strawberry yogurt, sprinkled with unsalted peanuts.

After she showered, Lorene dressed in a navy A-line dress with a dusty-blue open-front overlay, elbow-length sleeves and a sweetheart neckline. The hemline fell an inch above her knees, and her legs were highlighted by navy blue hose and matching shoes. Her only jewelry was diamond earrings and a wide-banded silver watch. She laid a lightweight white blazer on the bed and looked at her watch. Only one o'clock.

While she waited, she scanned a brochure Opal had sent from Pittsburgh about Jon Preston. Two years ago the boy had been an unknown high school student in Alabama, until he'd entered a music contest at the insistence of the school's music teacher. He won the contest and was instantly contacted by a recording company, but Preston's father had absolutely refused to permit his son to sign a contract until he graduated from high school. When Jon was allowed to make his own decision, he'd started recording and soon became famous throughout the country.

Preston was described as a passionate country newcomer, named as last year's Best New Male Country Artist. His most recent album, *New Kid on the Block,* was named after the title song that Preston had written himself.

As she read about Preston's rapid rise to fame, Lorene couldn't believe that he would agree to come to Woodston.

In spite of Lorene's anticipation, when Perry's

knock sounded she waited a full minute before she went to the door. Perry was dressed in a black suit, white shirt and silk tie. He handed her a florist's box.

Stepping inside the room, he leaned over and kissed her forehead. "Happy fortieth birthday, Lorene."

His words didn't summon the fretful nostalgic reaction her mother's greeting had prompted this morning.

She couldn't speak, and with shaking fingers she opened the box that held a dozen yellow roses, looking as fresh as if they'd just come from the garden. "You remembered!"

"Every year."

Sniffing the fresh fragrance of the roses, she said, "Thank you. I'll see if there's a vase in the apartment. If not, I'll borrow one from Dottie."

Pleased that he'd remembered not only her birthday, but also her favorite flower, Lorene felt her body tingle from the top of her head to the tips of her toes. She found an empty quart jar on a shelf in the kitchen cabinets.

"Not very elegant for such a lovely bouquet, but I'll buy something better. I saw several lovely antique vases at one of the shops on Front Street." She clipped off one of the buds, arranged the rest in the jar and set them on a table in the living room. With a bit of the greenery she fashioned a corsage with the single rosebud. In the bedroom she rummaged in her jewelry box and found a pin to fasten the corsage on her shoulder. The green and yellow stood out vividly on the navy blue background of her dress.

Going back to Perry, she put an arm around his waist and leaned her head on his shoulder. "Thanks, Perry. I'll admit that I've been dreading this over-the-hill birthday. I know it's just another day on the calendar and has nothing to do with my age, but I've been depressed about it anyway."

"It isn't just another day. We're going to celebrate this milestone in your life."

Perry didn't respond to her gesture of affection, and, feeling rebuffed, Lorene reluctantly moved away from him. What else could she expect?

"I'm ready to leave if you are," she said, going to the bedroom for her purse.

Perry saw the hurt look on her face as she turned away, and he also experienced a poignant emotional yearning. But after he'd yielded to the impulse to ask Lorene to dinner, he'd had second thoughts. He was getting along very well as it was. He had a rewarding life, and he'd thought the path for his future was settled until Lorene had reentered his life. He reminded himself daily that in a few weeks she'd return to her job in Pittsburgh. And then what would he have? A shattered heart, as he'd had before when she left him? A void in his life that no one except Lorene could fill?

At first Perry had been thankful that God had re-united him and Lorene, but as he'd fought a daily battle with his emotions, he believed it would have been better if he'd never seen her again. He didn't want to be in love with Lorene. But did love ever die? Once in love, was it forever? There were lots of troubling questions, but no answers.

As Perry watched Lorene walk toward him, lovelier and more tempting than she'd been as a girl, he knew his heart was in trouble. He must exert all possible discipline to keep her at arm's length.

At midnight, when they returned to Woodston, Perry walked to the apartment door with Lorene.

"Want to come in for a while?" she invited.

"No. I've a busy day tomorrow."

"Thanks for giving me a lovely birthday. It's a relief to know I won't have to dread my fortieth anymore," she said with an attempt at humor. "Thanks, Perry."

"My pleasure," he said. "Both of us needed a break from the bicentennial." He reached for her right hand and gave it a slight squeeze. "I'll be in touch tomorrow."

She stood at the door and listened to his receding footsteps. The fragrance of the yellow roses mocked her when she entered the apartment. Without removing her dress, she spread out, facedown, on the bed, more despondent than she'd been this morning. On the surface, they'd had an enjoyable evening, but something was missing.

Perry had taken her to a lavish restaurant on the

outskirts of Louisville. They'd dined on hors d'oeuvres, a melon-ball cup, T-bone steaks, browned potato balls, stuffed mushrooms with Brazil nuts, broccoli Polonaise, mixed green salad with a special dressing of olive oil and herbs, and had enjoyed baked Alaska for dessert.

They'd talked nonstop about her efforts to start a media business and how it had prospered. He'd talked about the outstanding opportunities he had at Woodston College. They'd covered their families' histories for the past twenty years. Perry had been as affable and compelling as always, but something was missing.

When she'd first come to Woodston he'd seemed keen to build a new relationship on the mistakes of the past. Tonight there hadn't been a hint that he expected anything more from her than friendship. Lorene flopped over on her back, with her hands behind her head. She wished she could cry away her hurts and frustrations, but she stared at the ceiling dry-eyed. She was too dejected for tears.

Whereas her twentieth birthday was the best one she'd ever had, she knew she'd remember the fortieth as her worst. Her fears of reaching this milestone in her life had been justified. Perry had realized they had no future together, and it was breaking her heart all over again.

Chapter Seven

To leave Lorene standing at the door, her dejection evident in the droop of her shapely shoulders, was one of the hardest things Perry had ever done. "God forgive me," he whispered as he drove away from the B and B. "I didn't want to leave her at all." Perry had thought that time would have diminished such impulses, but a few hours in Lorene's company had proven how wrong his assumption had been.

All evening he'd fought the urge to revive the intimacy they'd once had, exerting all the willpower he could muster to keep their relationship impersonal. He strongly suspected that it was up to him— that Lorene was more vulnerable than he was, and if he relented at all, they could be on shaky ground very easily. He'd failed Lorene once by being too impetuous, and he wouldn't do it again.

Perry's desperation drove him to his knees. Arriving at his home, he entered a small windowless room, free from outside distraction, where he often went to pray. Kneeling beside an old rocking chair that had belonged to his grandfather, who'd been a preacher, he bowed his head on the cushioned seat. He cherished the chair because it reminded him of the Christian heritage he'd received from his ancestors.

Perry didn't voice a petition to God, for his distress was so keen he didn't even know how to pray. Right now he needed a message from God to guide him in dealing with his feelings about Lorene. He was only human, and in spite of all his forebodings about what grief might come from loving her, tonight he loved Lorene with all his humanness.

In times like these, Perry relied upon the assurance from the book of Romans when the apostle Paul had said, "We do not know what we ought to pray, but the Spirit Himself intercedes for us with groans that words cannot express."

Usually Perry knew in advance what he should do and asked God to bless his decisions. Now he was helpless. Suddenly the situation of David entered his mind, and he believed God had sent him a message. David was one of the few Old Testament people of whom God had said, "He's a man after My own heart." David was far from being perfect, and one of *his* sins had been committing adultery with Bathsheba.

Still on his knees, Perry opened the Bible lying

on the small table by his chair. He turned to Psalm 51, written by David after his sin with Bathsheba and the resulting death of her husband. He read a portion of the psalm aloud.

"'Have mercy on me, O God, according to Your unfailing love; according to Your great compassion blot out my transgressions. Wash away all my iniquity and cleanse me from my sin.'"

Perry remembered he'd read that same Scripture before he and Lorene had agreed that they should discontinue their intimate relations. He'd believed that God had forgiven him for his youthful transgression, and from that time on he'd followed God's leading as much as possible. Although he'd known he was doing God's will, it had been a lonely life. Even now he experienced God's forgiving love over that incident, but as David had to do, Perry knew he was suffering the consequences of what he'd done years ago.

Looking again at the psalm, he read, "Restore to me the joy of Your salvation and grant me a willing spirit to sustain me."

Perry sat in the chair and rocked slowly back and forth, waiting for God to speak. Dawn was approaching when he wearily went to bed. He'd come to the conclusion that God didn't frown on his desire to seek Lorene's company. He also believed that God would give him the strength to be her friend and not go too far along roads that would be displeasing to Him.

* * *

Lorene had never liked costume parties, but she thought she should dress the part to participate in Woodston's festivities. The Monday following her birthday, still without a costume, Lorene approached Alma Denney at her college office to see where she could find some pioneer garments.

"Most Woodston residents have been working for over a year on clothes to wear during Heritage Week," Alma said, "so it's a little late for you to find anything suitable. You can rent costumes in Louisville, but that's a long way to go. Besides, they're expensive. Dottie's a good seamstress. Why not ask her if she can come up with something for you?"

"She's so busy. I don't want to impose on her."

"Dottie loves to sew, and she says she can relax better at the sewing machine than anywhere else."

Perry came into the office while they were talking, seemingly as friendly as always, so maybe she'd imagined his reticence on her birthday.

"What kind of costume do you have for the parade?" Lorene asked.

"A *gen-u-wine*—" he drawled the word "—Dan'l Boone outfit." His eyes crinkled with laughter. "Coonskin cap and all."

"I think," Alma said, "that you can buy a gingham bonnet at the craft store on Front Street. I figure Dottie could make a dress for you in a hurry."

"I'll buy a bonnet and see what else I can get at

the craft store before I ask her." She started toward the door. "And I'd better get started on it. See you later."

"On Monday of Heritage Week I'm supposed to help pole a flatboat into Woodston," Perry said, detaining her. "Some of us are practicing on the river behind Alma's house tonight. I'm not much of a sailor—want to come and watch me fall in the river?"

"Sure. What time?"

Perry looked at Alma, and she said, "Around seven o'clock."

"I'll stop by and pick you up," Perry said.

"All right. I'm going shopping now, but call before you come. When I get back to the apartment, I might have enough voice mail and e-mail messages to keep me busy the rest of the night."

Perry's longing gaze followed her out the door, and when he noticed Alma watching him, the sudden rush of color to his face contrasted sharply with his gray hair and mustache.

"Sometimes I wonder just how *well* you and Lorene knew each other."

"We were both enrolled in the school of engineering, and we had several classes together. We were friends."

But as he went into his office, he wondered how many other people besides Alma had noticed an unusual depth to their relationship. Try as he might, he couldn't be impersonal when he was with Lorene.

Her presence stirred his blood like a full glass of sassafras tea in springtime.

Mulling over Perry's attitude today compared to what it had been on her birthday, Lorene's mind was only half on her shopping, but she found a bonnet and a hand-crocheted shawl at one of the craft shops along the river.

When she returned to Riverview Ridge, she knocked on the door to Dottie's living quarters. She and John were eating lunch, and she insisted that Lorene should eat with them.

"No, I can't do that," Lorene said. "I didn't realize you were eating or I wouldn't have bothered you. I'll come back later."

Taking Lorene by the arm, Dottie pulled her into the apartment. "Nonsense! You aren't bothering us."

John was a quiet man, and Lorene wondered if he was quiet by nature or if his natural personality had receded into the background after fifty years of living with his effusive wife. But the few times she'd seen them together she'd noticed that when John talked, Dottie listened.

"Stop tugging on her arm, Dottie," he said, and his wife obeyed him. "But do come in, Lorene. We're practically finished. Take time to have a glass of tea."

Lorene sat in the chair John indicated. He was broad shouldered and well muscled, still carrying the physique of a more youthful man. He had a mane of iron-gray hair, and Lorene figured that Perry would look like that by the time he was John's age.

Why did everything remind her of Perry? Her days would be a lot easier if she could put Perry out of her mind!

When Dottie set the tea in front of her, Lorene said, "I'm looking for a costume for the parade, and Alma suggested you might be able to provide something for me. I bought a bonnet and shawl, but couldn't find anything else in the stores."

"Sure. I can make one for you," Dottie said. "I've made costumes for several people. I have a one-size-fits-all pattern, and I can adapt it to your figure."

"What kind of fabric should I buy?"

"No need for you to go shopping," John said, chuckling. "Dottie's got enough material to start a fabric store. You can choose something from her shelves."

Lorene glanced at Dottie, who nodded. "That's right. If you like any of the material I have, it will save you some time."

"If you can make one garment for me to wear in the parade, I'll telephone the costume store in Louisville and rent a couple of dresses for Heritage Week. They can ship them to me."

Dottie's sewing room was located near the kitchen. When the two women entered, Lorene saw that one wall was lined with shelves full of fabric.

"I can't resist buying materials," Dottie admitted. "John says it's an addiction, and sometimes I think it is, too. But I love to sew, and it's handy to have material at my fingertips when I get the urge to make something."

Dottie had a length of material that matched the green gingham of Lorene's bonnet, and she said it wouldn't be any problem to have it ready for the parade.

"There's no shape to these things," Dottie said, "and I can make the dress in a couple of hours. Pioneer women wore serviceable clothes, so I won't have to put many frills on it."

"Thanks a lot," Lorene said. "I'll go upstairs and get busy. I'm going to the Denney home this evening, and I have several things to do before then."

"We'll be there, too. John's in charge of the flat-boat expedition."

Twenty or more people had gathered on the riverbank behind the Denney home when Perry and Lorene arrived.

"Hey," Zeb called. "We're waiting on you."

Laughing, Perry said, "Frankly, I delayed, hoping you'd be finished by the time we got here. I don't know why I let myself get pressured into this expedition."

Two oblong wooden flatboats, thirty by fifty feet, were tied to Zeb's fishing dock. Each boat had a small boxlike structure in the middle, with four long poles lying on the deck. John Montgomery was walking around the deck of one of the boats, wearing an orange life preserver.

Dottie sidled over to Lorene, saying nervously, "He doesn't have a clue to what he's supposed to be doing. He can't even swim. Had a fit when I told him he *had* to wear a life jacket. I didn't convince him until I started talking about all the things my next husband and I could do with his life insurance."

Lorene laughed with Dottie, who could always be expected to bring a bit of levity to any occasion.

When Dottie said, "I'd better go closer and give him some more advice," and hustled toward the river, Lorene rolled her eyes toward Perry. "You'd better wear a life jacket, too."

"I'm not afraid of drowning, nor even that the crafts might sink. They were made by an excellent boat manufacturer. But I *am* afraid of ending up in New Orleans. This river is a lot deeper and swifter than it was when rafts and flatboats were first used. Once we start downstream, we might have trouble controlling the boats."

Zeb heard Perry's remark and said, "There's no chance of that. See those little huts in the middle of the boats?"

Perry nodded.

"They're camouflage for two powerful motors that will operate propellers underneath the flatboats. We'll be poling for historical flavor, but engineers will be inside the little buildings keeping everything under control.''

"Then let's go. What are we waiting for?" Perry said.

"Until the river is free of commercial craft. There's a towboat coming upstream, and it won't pass for another fifteen minutes."

"Gather down here," John shouted in a deep voice as loud as a foghorn. When everyone stood close to the riverbank, he continued, "All we intend to do is crisscross the river a few times tonight. The flatboats will be anchored here at Zeb's landing for safekeeping until Heritage Week. Then we'll take them upriver for a couple of miles and float downstream to make a grand entrance at the fort, half a mile below here."

"Are you feeling adventurous?" Perry asked Lorene in a teasing voice. "To make it authentic, some ladies should ride on the flatboats."

Diesel engines heralded the arrival of the towboat as its barges came in sight at the curve in the river. "Get ready," John shouted. "We'll have an hour before another boat comes down the river."

"I'm going along," Dottie said. "John may need my advice," she added, laughing.

"I'll go, too." Lorene said. "But I want a life preserver. I'm not a good swimmer."

"They're on the platform," Perry said. "Plenty for everyone."

Waves generated by the powerful towboat washed

against the bank, and John wouldn't let anyone board until the water was calm again.

Holding Perry's hand, Lorene walked carefully down the gangplank to the smooth deck of the flatboat. Wooden barrels and cartons were scattered on the deck, and several bales of rope were piled in the corner. In spite of these efforts to portray authenticity, Lorene doubted that the pioneers had transportation as comfortable as this flatboat.

"These things must have cost a lot of money," she mentioned to Perry when they were safely on board.

"They're rented by the manufacturer for events like this. We're only paying a nominal fee to use the flatboats."

Zeb Denney was crew master of the boat Perry and Lorene were on, but Alma had stayed behind to prepare refreshments.

"Okay," John shouted from the second vessel. "Zeb, get your men in place and prepare to take off. I'll wait until you've made a round trip before we start."

Lorene sat on a wooden bench beside the hut, facing forward. The hum of the small diesel engine was audible. With the men acting as if their poles made the raft move, the little engine took them back and forth across the river smoothly and without incident. Each flatboat made several practice trips before John heard via his cell phone that they had to clear the river.

The men gathered in the Denneys' backyard to discuss the few glitches they'd encountered and how to overcome them. Dottie and Lorene helped Alma place sandwiches, cookies and colas on the picnic table.

As dusk fell, Lorene sat on the ground and leaned against the trunk of a maple tree, nibbling on a sandwich. She'd never been talkative in a crowd, always uncomfortable in large groups, but she was enjoying herself tonight. Most of these people were connected with the college and had a close fellowship based upon their attendance at the chapel services there. Lorene had never taken part in the social events of the churches she'd attended, but she could see now that she'd probably missed an important aspect of church life.

Perry circulated, talking to everyone, but he often looked in Lorene's direction, wanting to be with her. Finally he picked up two glasses of cola and brought one to her.

"Want anything else before I sit down?" he asked.

"Some dessert would be nice."

He put several brownies on a plate and came back to lounge on the ground beside her.

"Peaceful, isn't it?" Lorene said. "I can see why Alma likes it."

"I like it, too—I'm glad I have a standing invitation to come here."

Dottie started singing a hymn, and she was soon

joined by others, but neither Lorene nor Perry sang. Lorene wasn't familiar with the song, and Perry had always said he'd been behind the door when singing talents were passed out. They sat shoulder to shoulder, quietly enjoying the spiritual warmth and love among these friends. If this evening was an example of Perry's present lifestyle, Lorene decided it would be a good life to share.

As Perry drove her back to the apartment, she said, "I'm being introduced to a whole new way of life in Woodston, and I can see lots of advantages in small-town living."

"Such as?"

"I'm making friends. I'm a loner and have never gotten close to others. I know lots of people, but when my workday is over, I pull the walls of my house around me and shut out the rest of the world. I'm beginning to see what I've missed."

When they arrived at Riverview Ridge, Perry walked to the door with her.

"Let me come in for a minute," he said. "I have an overwhelming urge to kiss you, and I don't want to do it on the porch. Dottie has keen eyes."

He held her elbow lightly as they climbed the stairs. The room was faintly illuminated by a small lamp in the bedroom. Perry put his arm around Lorene's waist, drew her toward him, and she relaxed in his embrace. She touched his cheek in a wistful gesture. She sensed his warm breath on her face before his lips moved over hers. The kiss was provocative and raised a question between them that had no answer.

He put her away gently. "Good night, sweetheart," he said, backing out the door. Lorene stood with trembling hands pressed to her lips. She didn't answer as she locked the door behind him.

Chapter Eight

Although Perry believed that God had forgiven him for the lapse of morality with Lorene, it still bothered him that he hadn't been strong enough to curb his emotions when they'd been in college. He took full blame for it, and he knew that even now he'd feel better about the situation if he and Lorene got married. But how would she feel about that? It had always seemed that something was missing in his life, and, despite all of her success, he didn't believe Lorene was completely satisfied, either. When they were together, the old emotional spark flamed just as it had years ago, so perhaps marriage was the answer. Once married, Lorene might tell him why she'd deserted him, the past could be erased and they'd find true love again. The more he thought about it, the more he believed that was the right thing to do.

Alma invited both of them for dinner the following Sunday evening, and Perry intended to take the opportunity to talk to Lorene privately.

He was further convinced that marriage was the answer to their problem when circumstances seemed to advance his purpose. Upon their arrival at the Denney home, Alma said crossly, "My oven timer didn't start, so we can't eat for an hour. Go, sit on the boat dock and watch the world go by. I'll call you when it's time."

"I'll stay and help," Lorene responded. "You shouldn't have to do all the work."

"Shoo," Alma said, waving her arms toward the river. "Everything is ready except the chicken casserole, and I'll have to wait on it. I'm cranky now, so I won't be good company."

Perry and Lorene walked toward the river without talking. When they were seated in two white chairs facing the river, Lorene said, "I'm glad to have a short breather. My current situation is sort of like Alma waiting on the casserole. Except for receiving Jon Preston's confirmation, I've done everything I can until the last minute. Then boom I'll have to pull all the loose ends together in a short time. I only pray I haven't forgotten something."

"I'm glad to have this time with you, too. I've been thinking and praying about something the past two days, hoping I'd get a chance to speak to you. Alma's predicament made this easy for me, so I take that as a good sign. Lorene, let's get married."

Lorene's eyes widened, and she stared at him as if she hadn't seen him before. Then her green eyes narrowed and hardened.

"Excuse me!" she said, adding incredulously, "What did you say?"

"Let's get married. I don't see why that should surprise you so much."

"Just like that! Let's get married, without any discussion?"

Obviously she didn't like the idea, and Perry was disgruntled. Just when he thought he was doing the right thing, Lorene's anger flared up. Belatedly he remembered that he'd made this decision without praying about it.

"I didn't mean to upset you, but it just seems the right thing to do. I've always blamed myself for pushing our relationship too far, and I'd feel better about myself if you were my wife. We were engaged once, so you apparently wanted to marry me then."

Why did he suspect that the longer he talked the more angry Lorene became?

Lorene's heart thumped a little faster at the mere thought of being married to Perry. She'd wanted him to be her husband for years, so why not take what he offered? But there had been no mention of love. When she'd first come to Woodston, emotional sparks had sizzled between her and Perry, but occasionally he displayed an aloofness that troubled her.

"So you want to get married to make a chaste woman of me?"

After they sat in silence for several minutes, Perry said, "I didn't mean it that way. Of course, I'm assuming a lot—maybe you don't want to marry me."

"Let's get one thing straight. As far as blame is concerned, you didn't force me into anything I didn't want to do." She was very angry with him, but she didn't take the time to consider why this was so. Was now the time to tell him everything? Tell him the main reason she couldn't marry him?

"Once we were compatible," Lorene chose to say instead, "but I don't know that we are now. Too many things have changed. You have your career, and I have mine. However, I'll be honest with you. The old emotional pull is still there, but I sometimes think we're only chasing rainbows to believe we can take up where we left off years ago."

He bent toward her. "There's one way we can find out. I don't think Alma and Zeb will be watching us very closely, and there's no one on the river." He put an arm around her shoulders and turned her face toward him. The pressure of his lips filled Lorene with a sense of longing. He kissed her closed eyelids, then the tip of her nose, and finally reached her lips in a demanding kiss that brought the past rushing headlong into the present. Her heart soared with unbidden memories. In a blinding moment, re-membrance of the happiness she'd once known in

Perry's arms melted most of the reservations she had about marrying him. But there were *some* reservations, and she drew slowly away.

His dark eyes gleamed at her, and she lifted a hand and smoothed his gray hair, ruffled by the breeze from the river. "Thanks for making me remember, Perry. We were happy together once, weren't we? Maybe that time will come again, but there's too much going on now to know what to do."

He sighed and leaned back in his chair. "I know. We have this celebration to promote."

"It isn't only that." She hesitated. "Is there any such thing as an unpardonable sin?"

He turned a startled gaze toward her, and at that inopportune moment Zeb called from the back porch. "Hey, people. Dinner's ready."

"Forget I said that," Lorene said, standing wearily. "Life would be much simpler if we could just stay here and let the rest of the world go by."

Perry drew her close, gave her a gentle hug and kissed the top of her head. There was a trace of laughter in his voice when he said, "Ah, that's the problem! And I don't have an answer to that one."

Although the bicentennial was mentioned briefly, most of the evening's conversation centered on some of Zeb's more humorous exploits as police chief in Woodston. Lorene was glad to be away from the pressures of the celebration for a few hours, and listening to Zeb reminisce kept her from considering Perry's proposal.

"This is my last year as chief," he said with some regret. "I turn sixty-five in November, and that's as long as I can stay on the force." With a broad grin, he added, "I'm kinda looking forward to it, though. I'll spend a lot of time fishing down on the dock, I suspect."

"I don't doubt that," Alma said. With a mischievous glint in her eye, she added, "I'm going to have less money and more husband. I don't know how I'll handle that."

"You'd ought to be used to it by now," Zeb retorted, "after forty years of wedded bliss."

Alma answered him with a snort as she cleared the table to bring in dessert.

Lorene had soon learned that the good-natured heckling between Alma and Zeb was their way of showing affection. It had taken many years of love and companionship to develop such devotion. Lorene closed her eyes, her heart aching with pain, realizing that she and Perry had missed the tender years of young love, where they could have bonded through child rearing, financial struggles and dreams. It took all of those things to achieve a mature love and trust that nothing could shake. Alone, they'd become successful in their own professions, but how much more satisfying their lives would be if they could have shared their youth! While it might be possible for her and Perry to build a life on the ashes of their past mistakes, she mourned the years when Perry hadn't been a part of her life.

She opened her eyes and met Perry's glance across the table, grief and despair shattering her heart. Did his face reflect the same sense of loss and anguish she felt? It seemed as if he could read her mind, knowing exactly what she was thinking, for unspoken pain glimmered in his dark eyes, too. Their hands clenched across the table in an electric moment when emotional vibes bounced back and forth from one hurting heart to the other.

The spell was broken when Alma called from the kitchen, "Who wants coffee with their apple pie?"

Lorene shook her head and glanced apologetically toward Zeb, who sat between her and Perry in embarrassed silence.

"Sorry," she said, and he nodded understandingly as Perry released her hand.

When Alma entered the room with a tray of desserts, she looked from one to the other, perhaps sensing an emotional undercurrent. Lorene thought that her face probably looked as strained as Perry's, so she wasn't surprised when the forthright Alma slapped the pie plates in front of them with unusual vigor, and said, "I know this isn't any of my business…"

"Now, Alma," Zeb started, but she forestalled him with an uplifted hand.

"It's plain as the nose on Zeb's face—you two

are so much in love it's tearing you apart. Why don't you get married and stop being miserable?''

Zeb laughed in his slow way. ''Alma, stop being a buttinsky, although the same idea has crossed my mind.'' And with a pert look at his wife, he added, ''Not that there aren't miserable moments when you're married, too.''

Perry glanced at Lorene, but her expression was unreadable. ''It's not as simple as it sounds,'' he said slowly.

Alma stepped behind Lorene and laid a hand on her tense shoulders. ''I shouldn't have said anything, but something happened years ago that's keeping you apart. And when my friends are unhappy, I am, too.''

''Thanks, Alma. Just pray for us to make right decisions,'' Lorene said. ''That's all you can do.''

They drove in silence back to Riverview Ridge, where Perry parked underneath the security light, so he could watch Lorene's expression. ''I want to know what you meant about the unpardonable sin,'' he said.

''Have you ever committed a sin you thought God wouldn't forgive?''

Her words surprised him, and he lifted his eyebrows questioningly. ''I've doubted at times, but no, I don't believe I've ever committed a sin that couldn't be forgiven. Why do you ask?''

"Oh, I heard a sermon once on the unpardonable sin, and I've often wondered what it is."

"No minister should preach a sermon on that subject and leave his hearers without a sound explanation." He rubbed his chin. "Do you think you've committed an unpardonable sin?"

Without meeting his gaze, she said in a quiet voice, "I don't know."

"But, Lorene—" Perry started.

She interrupted him. "You're a Bible scholar. Just tell me what the unpardonable sin is."

"Talk to a dozen different people about the subject, and you'll get a dozen different answers. But to the best of my knowledge and understanding, God will forgive any sin except refusing to acknowledge Him as Lord and Jesus as Savior."

"And that's all?"

He smiled. "Well, that requires quite a lot of commitment!"

She opened the door. "Thanks, Perry. It's been quite a day." When he started to get out of the car, she said, "No need for you to walk me to the door. I'll be fine."

She'd slammed the emotional door. He knew there wasn't any need to question her further.

"Do you want to run tomorrow morning?"

"No. I have to call Pittsburgh at eight o'clock for a consultation with Opal, and I might be pressed for time."

He watched until she entered the house. He

agreed that it had been quite a day, and he didn't know if his relationship with Lorene was more solid or on a more shaky foundation after his obviously unwelcome proposal. He wished she'd opened up and told him what she meant by the unpardonable sin. What nasty secret did Lorene harbor? What could she have done that was so wicked she believed God wouldn't forgive?

If Perry's explanation of the unpardonable sin was true, then Lorene's mind was calm on one point. Even at her lowest ebb, she'd never rejected God or doubted her eternal salvation. Lorene paused when she entered the apartment, leaned against the door and thanked God that He'd forgiven the mistakes of her youth. God had forgiven her, but would Perry?

As she prepared for bed, Lorene thought of Perry's proposal. She believed he was sincere in wanting to marry her, but she feared it was for the wrong reason. He hadn't told her he loved her. But why else would he have remained a bachelor? Did she still love him? If she didn't, wouldn't she have married someone else long before now? But how about her job? After she'd worked so hard to reach the position she held now, would she give that up to move to a small town? Despite the puzzling questions, Lorene drifted off to sleep, but she didn't rest. She kept waking from a dream where she reached for Perry, and he constantly eluded her outstretched arms.

The next morning Lorene worked on the computer, making last-minute contacts with television networks before talking to Opal about negotiations with Jon Preston's agent. After a brisk walk to the river, she ate a late breakfast, and didn't stop working to have lunch. In midafternoon a knock on her door startled her from her concentration. She opened the door to see her mother and father standing in front of her, grinning widely.

"Surprise!" Celeste Harvey shouted.

It wasn't a surprise—it was a nightmare! Hoping her panic at this unexpected visit didn't show on her face, Lorene said, "Come in. It *is* a surprise."

Lorene had gotten her physical appearance and temperament from her mother, whose carefully tended features belied Celeste's sixty-five years. Celeste was mild mannered, often cowed by her aggressive husband, Addison—a tall, rawboned man with grayish hair, a few years older than Celeste.

Asking them to join her in the living room, Lorene said, "You'd mentioned that you might come to the bicentennial observance, but that isn't until next week."

"Your father was worried about you being down here alone, so we decided to come early to check on you, and then spend a few days searching out his family's ancestry in Kentucky. We'll be back in time for the big celebration. We've been seeing advertisements about it on television."

A cold knot formed in Lorene's stomach at the

prospect of her parents spending that much time in Woodston, so she ignored that part of her mother's comments. "I hoped we'd get good television coverage on the event. Have you had lunch? I'm living light here, but I can fix a sandwich and drink for you."

"We've already had our lunch," Addison said. He looked over the apartment while Celeste admired the view of the river. "Well, I guess this place is all right," he said, "but I wanted to be sure."

Lorene had long ago stopped stewing about her father's assumption that she wasn't capable of running her own life, so she ignored his comment.

"We've taken a motel room for tonight and then we'll move on tomorrow," he said.

"You're welcome to stay here. You can have the bedroom, and I'll sleep on the couch. It makes a comfortable bed." Lorene had an uncontrollable urge to keep her eyes on her parents while they were in Woodston.

"No need for that," he said. "I didn't think much of the motel room, but it'll do for overnight. I'll find something better when we spend several days here during Heritage Week."

"It's too late to reserve a motel in Woodston for next week. The motels are booked solid."

"We'll find a place," Addison said confidently. "Don't you have enough clout to find a room for us?"

"I don't have any clout in Woodston," she said

with a laugh. "I'm here to do a job, for which my agency is being paid. That doesn't give me much influence. But if you don't find a room for the celebration, you can stay in the apartment."

She'd promise them anything to get them out of Woodston before they encountered Perry. She didn't know how she could possibly prevent their meeting if they came back for Heritage Week, but perhaps they'd change their mind and return home without returning to Woodston.

"We'll take you out for dinner," Celeste said.

"That'll be fine. Since there aren't many restaurants in Woodston, let's go to Evansville for dinner."

Exerting all the discipline possible, Lorene was upbeat all evening, determined that her parents wouldn't suspect any problem and start probing. Although she had lots of unfinished work, Lorene prolonged their return to Woodston until after dark. The evening passed pleasantly enough, and since her parents were leaving the next morning, Lorene went to bed believing she'd kept them away from Perry for the time being.

She wouldn't have been so confident if she could have seen the angry-faced man stalking up the walk toward Perry's house the next morning.

Chapter Nine

After he returned from exercising in the park, Perry showered, dressed in shorts and a knit shirt, and was preparing a light breakfast when the doorbell rang. Something about the caller seemed familiar, but Perry failed to recognize the man's voice when he growled, "I want to talk to you."

Perry unlatched the screen door and made a sweeping motion with his arm. "Come in."

The stranger barged into the living room and turned to fix Perry with a hostile stare. "I've waited a long time to tell you what I think of you. Now that I've accidentally found you in this town, we're going to have a long-overdue confrontation."

The man's attitude annoyed Perry, but he decided to listen. He sat on the arm of the sofa and motioned his visitor to a chair.

"Won't you sit down?"

"No! I can say what I want to standing up."

"Suit yourself," Perry said, shrugging his shoulders. "Why don't you come to the point? I don't even know who you are."

"Addison Harvey! Does that mean anything to you?"

Shocked, but trying to be conciliatory, Perry said, "Certainly, but I haven't seen you for a long time, Mr. Harvey. I'm sorry I didn't recognize you."

He stood again and extended his right hand, which Mr. Harvey ignored. What had brought Lorene's father to Woodston? And what had happened to cause his anger? The last time he'd seen the man was the time he'd gone to the Harvey home to support Lorene while she told her parents she'd withdrawn from engineering school. Mr. Harvey had resented Perry's influence on his daughter, but surely he hadn't harbored that anger for so many years.

"I made up my mind that if I ever saw you again, I'd tell you off for getting my daughter pregnant."

Addison's vitriolic tirade continued for more than five minutes, while Perry sat like a person turned to stone, so shocked he couldn't have spoken if he'd wanted to. The bitter words bounced off his shoulders as if he wasn't hearing them, because the man's first statement had pierced his heart.

Knowing there wasn't any reasoning with Harvey, and since the man seemed angry enough to start throwing punches at any time, Perry lifted his hand.

"I've heard all I want to hear. Please leave my house."

Perry walked into his bedroom and closed the door, wondering if Lorene's father would try to follow him. He stood at the window until he saw Addison leave the house and drive away. He quickly exchanged his shorts for a pair of slacks and rushed out to his car.

Ten minutes later he reached Riverview Ridge, spoke briefly to Dottie and John, who were sitting on the back porch, and hurried up the stairs. The door stood ajar, but he knocked anyway.

Lorene was at the computer, and she called, "Who is it?"

"Perry."

She closed her e-mail and hurried to the door, a smile on her face.

"I want to come in," he said shortly.

She'd never seen Perry looking like this. Wondering what was wrong with him, she drew back into the living room and motioned toward a chair. He stepped inside, shutting the door behind him. With the door closed, the apartment would get hot in a hurry, so Lorene flipped on the air conditioner. When she turned to face him, she realized why Perry's appearance was so unusual. He was angry— very angry! She'd never seen him this angry before.

"What's wrong?" she asked.

"Why didn't you tell me you were pregnant when you left me?"

He hadn't once considered that her father had been lying, but suddenly he hoped that the man had been wrong. When the blood drained from Lorene's face and she stumbled blindly to the couch, he knew it was true.

"I didn't know it then," she said in words barely more than a whisper. "How did you find out?"

"Not from you, that's for sure. I learned it when your father paid me a visit this morning. Did you tell him where to find me?"

Somehow she found the courage to face him. "No! They stopped by last night, planning to leave Woodston this morning. I wanted them to leave before they knew you lived here. I didn't want them to see you."

"Why? Because you figured they'd tell me what you hadn't?"

She nodded woodenly. "They blamed you for it all, Perry. They wouldn't believe that I was as much to blame as you were."

"It seems that you have a lot of explaining to do, but first, answer another question. Where is our child?"

Tears blinded Lorene, and she cradled her head in trembling hands. "I don't know. I gave the baby up for adoption," she whispered brokenly.

"Boy or girl?"

"A boy," she whispered.

Perry's hand clenched and unclenched as he stalked around the small room. In passing, he knocked a plastic glass filled with orange juice off the sink counter and didn't even pause to pick it up. He stopped with his hand on the doorknob. Even the sight of her trembling shoulders failed to lessen his anger.

"Lorene, I thought nothing you could ever do or say would make me stop loving you, but the way I feel right now, I'm not sure I ever want to see you again."

Perry walked blindly out of the apartment, ignored John and Dottie, got in the car and drove heedlessly for miles along country roads, twice narrowly avoiding accidents. He wasn't alert enough to be driving, but he had to get away from people. He couldn't bear the thought of encountering anyone he knew.

Even before he'd met Lorene, he'd dreamed of marrying and having a family, especially a son. But he'd given up hope that he would ever have any children and had learned to live with the disappointment. He couldn't believe that Lorene had given birth to his son and given him away! How could he ever forgive her?

Lorene ignored the ringing phone at first, but, when it continued to ring, she reached for it.

"Lorene," her mother said. "We're ready to leave town now. We'll telephone again in a few days."

"Just a minute. I want to talk to Dad before you go."

"This isn't a good time to talk to him."

"I want to talk to him."

"Yes?" her father said gruffly when Celeste handed him the phone.

"How did you know Perry lived in Woodston?" Lorene demanded.

"I picked up a Heritage Week brochure in the motel lobby, and I saw his name listed on the commission board. It certainly made me feel proud of my daughter to find out you were still running after the man who ruined your life. When did you take up with him again?"

"I didn't know Perry lived here until I arrived in Woodston. And I don't appreciate you bawling him out about what happened a long time ago. I told you over and over that I was as much to blame as Perry."

"Makes no difference. I'd been wanting to tell him off for years."

"Then why didn't you take the opportunity to do it when he called repeatedly and tried to find me twenty years ago? If you'd told him I was pregnant, he'd have come to me right away. Why did you destroy the letters he wrote me and convince me that he didn't want me any longer? Why did you make me give up my son when Perry and I could have married and raised the child ourselves?"

Lorene broke the connection and left the receiver

off the cradle. She didn't want her parents to call again. She'd already said more than she should have. A nasty attitude toward her parents wouldn't change what had happened in the past.

But she was suddenly overwhelmed by the torment that had wrenched her heart for years. She shuddered and collapsed on the couch, giving way to the anguish of her loss. She'd not only lost her child, but now she'd lost Perry as well, and she was absolutely without hope. It had been a long time since she'd given way to a crying jag, but an hour passed and she was still crying. Her body was so taut that even the sound of the air conditioner grated on her nerves. What was she going to do?

The loss of her child had been the worst thing that had ever happened to her. She remembered, as if it were yesterday, holding that tiny baby in her arms for a moment before her parents came to take him away. She begged to keep the child, but arrangements for the adoption had been made months ago, and she'd signed the paper when the child was nothing more than an unwanted intrusion into her life. But during her pregnancy and the wretched twelve hours she'd been in labor, she'd bonded with the baby, and she didn't want to lose him. But her parents refused her pleas.

She didn't blame Perry for being angry, for she'd never forgiven herself for the action she'd considered an unpardonable sin.

* * *

Perry returned to Riverview Ridge more slowly than he'd approached it earlier in the day. When he'd finally calmed down, he knew he had to go back to Lorene. He couldn't get her white, anguished face from his mind. Lorene had never been a weepy woman, but when she occasionally did cry, her tears were like an artesian fountain that wouldn't dry. Giving up her child had probably caused her enough grief without having to endure the verbal abuse he'd hurled at her. He had no doubt she was crying now.

He climbed the stairs to her apartment with leaden feet, knocked and, when there was no response, turned the knob, opened the door and entered. Compassion tore at his heart when he saw her sprawled on the couch.

Not even looking to see who it was, Lorene waved a limp arm that dangled close to the floor. "Go away," she sniffled.

"No, I'm not going away," Perry said, and she quickly lifted her head, biting her lips in an attempt to control her sobs.

Perry sat beside Lorene and pulled her into a sitting position, supporting her in his arms. She hid her tearstained face on his shoulder while the convulsive sobs continued.

"I'm sorry for what I said to you. Please forgive me." Lorene noticed he didn't say he'd forgiven her.

With his chin on her head, Perry gently rocked her

back and forth, waiting for the storm to pass. As always, Lorene's tears ceased abruptly, and for several minutes she quietly enjoyed the feel of his arms around her.

"I'm all right now," she said at last. "Go on to work. You must have loads of work backed up at the office, with all the time you've spent on the bicentennial."

"I'm not leaving you for a while."

She reluctantly left his embrace, saying wearily, "We *should* talk. It will be a relief to tell you. I'll go wash my face—it feels hot and dry. Back in a minute." She was too heartsick to even hide her dreary face from him.

Perry grabbed a paper towel off the rack to wipe up the spilled orange juice, and, noting a loaf of bread on the cabinet, he said, "I haven't had any breakfast. Okay if I make some toast?"

Walking toward the bathroom, she said, "Help yourself. There's butter and jelly in the refrigerator. And you can make a pot of coffee if you want to."

"Do you want anything?"

"I had juice and a bagel earlier, but I'll make a cup of tea in a minute. My stomach can't take anything else right now."

Perry had prepared the coffeemaker and was standing beside the sink eating the toast when she returned. As she gently applied cream to her dusty-rose skin, he noticed it was still as blemish free as it had been when she was a girl. She placed a cup of water in the microwave and had a tea bag waiting by the time the water boiled.

Carrying a cup of coffee, Perry went to the couch, and when Lorene started to sit in the chair he reached out his hand. "Sit with me."

She shook her head. "It'll be easier if I stay over here. I should have told you about the baby as soon as we met, or perhaps made more of an effort to find you when I learned I was pregnant. But I was very sick the first few months." She closed her eyes, and a look of raw grief spread across her face. "I didn't have an easy pregnancy."

"And I wasn't there to help you through it! Like I told you, I *did* try to contact you. I telephoned, but you didn't return the calls. I wrote letters. I reached your father by phone one day and he told me you didn't want to see me again, and to stop bothering you. When I came to the house, your family had moved."

Bitterly she replied, "And all the time they were telling me that you didn't care enough about me to make contact. I should have known better, but you'll remember that I allowed my parents to dominate me. I did oppose them on one thing—they were determined that I'd have an abortion, but I absolutely balked. When they threatened to kick me and the child out of the house to make it on my own, I finally agreed to adoption. I hadn't even finished college—I didn't know how I could get a job to support myself and a baby. My parents were too proud to admit that their daughter had an illegitimate child. I knew they'd never relent, so I decided our child might be better off with someone who could afford to take care of him.''

"So that's the unpardonable sin you've committed?"

"Yes. I couldn't forgive myself for giving my baby away, so I naturally wondered if God had forgiven me."

"I'm convinced that God has forgiven our mistake of the past, and He isn't pleased when we keep dwelling on it. In one of the psalms we have the assurance, 'As far as the east is from the west, so far has He removed our transgressions from us.' God has forgotten what we did—we have to forget it also."

"It was a terrible thing for me to do."

"Why didn't you try to contact me after you got out on your own? You knew where my parents lived—you could have found me through them."

"Don't forget that my parents had convinced me that you'd rejected me. And after what I'd done, I figured that was even more reason you wouldn't want me in your life, so I decided to go it alone."

"I know it isn't any of my business, so don't answer if you'd rather not. But how *alone?* Hasn't there ever been anyone else?"

She met his eyes frankly. "I've had sporadic dates through the years, but when anyone became serious I backed off. I wouldn't consider marrying anyone with the load of guilt on my conscience. Besides, I couldn't get you out of my mind.''

He reached out his hand, and she came to sit beside him, nestling in the circle of his arm.

''There's been no one else for me, either.''

''How could a few innocent mistakes make such a mess of our lives?''

''Your parents have to shoulder part of the blame, too. If they hadn't thrown such a fit about our engagement and threatened to cut off your money if we got married, or if they'd allowed me to contact you when you knew you were pregnant, we'd have managed. I'd have quit school and gone to work if I'd known I had a child to support. I wouldn't have deserted you, Lorene.''

She lifted a hand and patted his face, and he kissed her fingers. ''I know that now.''

''Who adopted the child?''

''I don't know. I signed the papers, but my parents made all the arrangements before the baby was born.''

''And you've never tried to find out what happened to him? Even to know if he's living or dead?''

Lorene detected a hint of censure in his tone. She looked out the windows and stiffened in his embrace.

''I gave the baby away. It wouldn't have been fair to his adoptive parents to interfere.''

He massaged her back until she relaxed again.

"I wasn't being critical. I know it wasn't easy for you."

"If they hadn't let me see the baby and hold him for a few minutes, I might have gotten over losing him. But my baby's image is etched into my memory, and there's never a day I don't see his face. He had a little cleft running from his nose to his upper lip just like the one you have. When he would have reached the shaving age, I wondered if he complained about the trouble that blemish caused him like you always did."

He grinned. "That's the reason I started wearing a mustache."

"And I've never forgotten the soft covering of dark hair on his head, the tiny fingers and toes, the softness of him, the baby smell. As the years passed, every time I've seen a boy that was the same age ours would have been, I've wondered if he might be our child. Although I've always wished I could have kept him, I made the best I could out of life, and I've never tried to find out where he is. I signed the adoption papers giving my son to another woman, and it wouldn't be ethical to contact him now and say, 'You're *my* boy.' That family, wherever they are, has done for my child what I should have done. I will *not* interfere in his life."

"But what if they aren't taking care of him? What if he's in need? We're financially able to help him now. If you know the date of his birth and the hospital where he was born, we can find out who adopted him.''

"No, Perry, I don't want to do it. It isn't fair to his adoptive parents.''

"Look at it from another angle. If *you* were adopted, wouldn't you want to know?''

This question had often entered her mind. "I don't think so—especially if I'd been born out of wedlock and my mother had abandoned me.''

Hoping to change her mind, he tried to explain his feelings to her. "It's always been a disappointment to me that I couldn't marry and have a family. And now that I know I have a son somewhere, every young man I see, I'll wonder if he could be the one.''

"I'm convinced that if I ever see our son, I'll know him. The months I nurtured him in my body and those few minutes I held him in my arms created a bond between us that will last until the day I die.''

"If I promise I won't interfere if the boy has a good life, will you let me make a preliminary search? If he's well and happy, I'll back off, but if he's down and out, needing any kind of help, I want to know it.''

"You have as much right as I do to make decisions about him.'' Lorene acquiesced to his request. "But I'm opposed to it. And if you learn anything about our son, don't tell me. I'll be better off to continue not knowing, but always hoping I'll recognize him someday when I meet him unexpectedly.

I don't think I could bear to learn he's been mistreated and had a difficult life."

Reluctantly Lorene told him the name of the hospital and the date their child was born.

Perry looked at his watch. "It's almost noon. Do you want to go somewhere for lunch?"

She shook her head. "No, thank you. I'm not going anywhere until I'm sure my crying jag is over. Besides, I still feel nauseous."

"Ginger ale used to help," he said, and she flushed, pleased that he remembered so much about her. "If you don't have any, I'll go buy some for you."

"There's ginger ale in the cabinet. Do you want to stay for lunch?"

"I don't care about lunch, but I don't want to leave you."

"You must have lots to do at the college, and you don't need to stay with me. I'll be all right. Actually, it's a tremendous load off my mind that you know the truth at last. I should have told you, but I just couldn't."

Although he was still disappointed, and somewhat angry that she hadn't told him as soon as they'd been reunited, Perry nodded understandingly.

"The best thing for me to do is to work," Lorene stated. "I still have a few strings to pull trying to guarantee Jon Preston's appearance at the celebration, but it's pretty much confirmed. Opal is discussing arrangements with Preston's manager, and

I'll take care of the details at this end. If he agrees to come to Woodston, I won't have time to do much promotion, and I don't know where I can find a place for his concert. It will have to be a big place if Preston is as popular as Mr. Kincaid says."

"You don't have much choice. The high school auditorium won't hold more than five hundred people, and as I understand, thousands of people attend his concerts. The football stadium is the only place I know that's big enough to hold a large crowd."

"And that isn't very satisfactory in this heat, or if we should have inclement weather on the day of his concert. I don't know why Mr. Kincaid didn't realize that Jon Preston is too big a fish to swim in Woodston's pond. In a year's time, the young man has soared to the top of favorite country singers."

"Mr. Kincaid doesn't think Woodston is a small pond, and he believes money will buy anything."

"As a PR person, I have to get along with everyone, so I'm not going to quarrel with Mr. Kincaid, but I'll tell you frankly, I'll be glad when the next two weeks have passed and I've put Woodston's celebration behind me. In the meantime, let's try to pretend that you don't know any more about me than you did yesterday. I have to keep focused on the celebration, and I can't do that if I keep recalling unpleasant memories."

He put his arm around her shoulders and squeezed her gently. "Call if you need me," he said. He started to leave and turned back.

"I'm going to camp at the fort during Heritage Week. Why don't you plan to, also? It would be a good way to get in the thick of things. The Denneys and I are camping together. You and Alma can share a cabin, and Zeb and I can sleep in a tent."

"I should be there," Lorene agreed, "because that's where the action will be. Actually, most of my work will be over by then. If I haven't done a good promotion job by that time, it'll be too late."

In spite of the work she had to do, Lorene sat in the chair with her head bowed for a long time after Perry left. She was grateful that Perry had returned and apologized, but their conversation hadn't ended to Lorene's satisfaction. Perry had apologized for losing his temper and had comforted her. Still, he hadn't said that he forgave her for letting their son go. Lorene was convinced that the loss of their son was a barrier between her and Perry that could never be resolved.

Chapter Ten

Lorene put her sorrows of the past and the worries about the future behind her, determined to immerse herself completely in Woodston's bicentennial. Work could always take Lorene's mind off personal problems.

Her heart was at ease now that Perry knew about their son, and she was thankful that she'd been forced into telling him what had happened, but she was still angry at her father for the way he'd broken the news to Perry.

God, I know I should be a more dutiful daughter, but shouldn't Dad be willing to meet me halfway? He's never done that. And about Perry looking for our child—I would like to know where he is, too, but I don't want to interfere in his life unless it's for his own good. You know best, Father, and I'm learning to leave some things in Your hands, rather

than to try to fix everything myself. It's taken a long
time for me to learn that. Amen.

Comforted in spirit, if not in mind, she started to
work. When she accessed her e-mail, she saw she
had a message from Opal.

"Finally had a confirmation from Andy Preston,
who is not only Jon's father, but also his agent and
manager. They've agreed to present a concert in
Woodston on Sunday afternoon, the day after the
celebration ends. They require a guarantee of at least
ten thousand tickets, at forty dollars each. Do you
think Woodston can swing that? Let me know before I sign the contract and fax it back to them.
When I contact them again, I'll nail down how much
of that money Preston will demand."

"Wow!" Lorene shouted aloud. "$400,000. This
will cause Mr. Kincaid to sit up and take notice!"

Lorene telephoned Mr. Kincaid immediately, and
when she told him the terms, he was silent for at
least two minutes.

"That's taking quite a risk," he finally said.

"You don't have to agree. My associate hasn't
approved the contract yet."

"Can you bring in ten thousand people?"

Annoyed that he expected her to perform miracles
in such a short time, she said, "I don't know. We've
never promoted Preston, so I can't estimate how big
a crowd he'll draw. For other stars of his caliber,
we've started six months ahead of the scheduled appearance, and I don't know what I can do in less

than two weeks. I'll do what I can, but I won't guarantee that many people. There are lots of other problems, too. That's a bigger crowd than I anticipated, and I doubt the football stadium will hold them. And Zeb's police force isn't adequate to control so many people. I hate to keep harping on this, but you waited too late to invite a celebrity like Preston. I think you should wait and have him at another time."

"But this is the only time Woodston will celebrate its bicentennial," Kincaid said stubbornly.

"If you accept Preston's offer, I need to know right away."

"Let me make a few phone calls, and I'll get back with you."

"I'm leaving now to check on the football field, but I'll have my cell phone with me. I *must* know as soon as possible," she insisted.

Lorene had learned from Zeb and Alma that the county's high schools had consolidated three years earlier and a new building had been constructed to house the combined student body. Funds had been donated by a rich alumnus to finance the football field. The stadium was impressive—an unusually large facility for a small town, obviously built with population growth in mind.

Although she supposed Preston would bring in his own technicians and equipment, Lorene checked out the sound system with the football coach and found it more than adequate. The coach said the stadium's seating capacity was around eight thousand, but if folding chairs were placed on the football field itself, they could accommodate ten thousand people. And no doubt people would stand to hear Preston, but she asked the coach to check out the insurance coverage on an above-capacity crowd, and also to see if they'd be breaking any state safety codes to seat the audience on the field.

Lorene made sketches of the stadium, blocking in the location of Preston's stage. She'd have to find someone to erect the stage and a place to rent folding chairs. She'd also need to find out how many people would be in the performer's troupe—no doubt he'd have bodyguards, musicians and behind-the-scene helpers. Where in Woodston could she find room to house so many people? Some celebrities often traveled with a bigger staff than the president of the United States.

But Lorene actually welcomed all the pressure. Her adrenaline worked overtime when she was presented with a challenge. With the work ahead of her, she wouldn't have time to consider her own personal problems.

She hadn't been back in the apartment more than an hour when Mr. Kincaid telephoned.

"We've gone too far to back out now," he said, "so conclude the contract with Preston."

"I'll do that as soon as I bring in a revised contract for you to sign adding this concert to a list of our agency's duties and noting the additional expense.''

''Is that necessary?''

''Absolutely. I'll be there within an hour, and then I'll contact the Pittsburgh office and make the other arrangements. By the way, the football stadium will do nicely for the concert.''

''Glad to hear it,'' he said shortly.

She thought Mr. Kincaid's gruffness over her insistence on the contract was unwarranted, but she had learned never to take someone's word for a business deal. She had the contract signed by four o'clock, and she e-mailed a message to Opal.

''Go ahead and sign with Jon Preston. Find out what accommodations they'll expect and how many people travel with him. Remind Preston that Woodston is a small town, and we can't provide a ritzy environment. Thanks.''

Leaving the final closing with Preston up to her office staff, Lorene prepared for another televised interview with Reginald Peters—an event she had anticipated for days. Reginald was an eccentric in many ways, but also an interesting person. Lorene had liked him immediately, and she thought a tour of his home as he detailed the history of Woodston would likely be the zenith of her planned promotion.

Perry volunteered to take her to the Peters home, which was five miles southwest of Woodston. He picked Lorene up at one o'clock, and they stopped by the motel so Lorene's camerawoman could follow them to Stone Gate, the Peters estate.

"You're looking better this morning," he commented. "Did you sleep well last night?"

"Not bad. I'm always pumped up when my work goes well, and now that we know for sure that Jon Preston will appear in Woodston, I've gotten excited about it. At first I was angry that Kincaid pushed for this, but I'm happy about it now. I'll be so busy for the next two weeks that I won't think about anything except the bicentennial."

"Not even a thought for me now and then?" he asked, a teasing smile etching the corners of his mouth.

"Maybe, in my dreams."

"That will be enough, I suppose. If they're good dreams."

"Never any other kind," she assured him. "After I got over my hurt and disappointment, I realized how much I'd lost by leaving you. Since then, I've never had any bitter thoughts about you, Perry."

"I've had plenty of bitter thoughts about myself for not handling matters better, but it's in the past. Are you looking forward to today's interview?"

She noticed again that he changed the subject when they approached the whispers of the heart. Ignoring her disappointment, she answered evenly, "Very much."

The Peters mansion stood on a hill two miles from the Ohio River, high above the floodplain. They approached the house from the rear, but the road curved easily up the hill, and Perry paused on a promontory that presented a broad vista of the Ohio River Valley.

"Mr. Peters owns land on both sides of the river, so he's been able to control expansion that would destroy this view. He's dedicated to keeping this property as a memorial to his ancestors, and he doesn't want to change it."

Stone Gate was situated in the middle of an impressive five-acre lawn, landscaped with evergreens, shrubs and flowers that would have been fashionable when the house was built. A dovecote atop a white gazebo was the focal point of a large rose garden.

"What was Mr. Peters's profession? I know he's reached his retirement years now, but he must have worked sometime."

"He owns a thousand acres of prime farmland, and it's a full-time job taking care of that. He inherited enough wealth to enable him to stay home and be a good steward over his estate."

"Mr. Peters is a bachelor, isn't he? What happens to this place after he's gone?"

"He has no intention of going any time soon," Perry joked. "But what he intends to do with this property is a well-kept secret that only he and his lawyer know. The property is registered with the National Historic Landmark Association, governed by certain restrictions, no matter who owns it. I wouldn't be surprised if he wills everything to the Commonwealth of Kentucky as a perpetual monument to his family, but that's pure assumption.''

It was like a journey back in time to approach the Peters mansion. The date, 1780, was inscribed on the arch topping the stone entrance gate. When Reginald stepped off the columned gallery to welcome them, Lorene asked, ''Surely this house wasn't built in 1780?''

''No. That's the year my ancestor settled on this land. He lived in a log cabin at first. Over the next hundred years the family increased their holdings and accumulated wealth. Our estate was spared any destruction during the War Between the States when the Peters men fought for the Union. My great-grandfather married a Northern heiress after the war, and they used her money to increase his land holdings and build this house. She had always enjoyed gracious living, and she wanted the house to reflect her position in society. Until she married into our clan, the Peters had been a rough lot, accustomed to frontier living, but she took the rough edges off the family.''

The house had fourteen rooms, eight of which were in the square original structure. In later years a two-story wing had been added with six more rooms. According to the custom of the time, the kitchen had been separated from the main house by a covered walkway.

''In my father's day,'' Reginald explained, ''the

walkway was enclosed with windows for winter weather, and made into a screened breezeway during the summer. Our food is still prepared in the original kitchen that was modernized years ago.''

For his video interview Reginald sat in an upholstered Queen Anne chair, with side wings, wooden legs and wooden hand rests, below the huge portraits of his ancestors who had built the home. With his mop of gray hair, his rugged features and his piercing brown eyes, he was a picturesque sight. Lorene could tell that the photographer was delighted with Reginald's responses and his appearance.

After the camerawoman left to edit the tape for Lorene's approval, Reginald insisted that Lorene and Perry take light refreshments with him. They joined him in wooden rocking chairs on the side veranda that overlooked the river valley. Because there was a long curve in the Ohio at that point, the river could be seen from almost any window at Stone Gate.

The maid had just brought them a dish of sherbet, cookies and iced tea when Lorene's phone rang. She excused herself and stepped to the far side of the veranda to answer.

''Hello,'' her office manager said. ''Everything is all set with the Prestons. Their advance people—sound men, photographers, choreographers—travel in trailers and motor homes, so you'd have to arrange parking for them. Jon and his close associates travel in vans and will require rooms for ten people.

Can you manage that? Actually, this guy seems to be down-to-earth, and I don't believe he'll be fussy about his lodgings.''

"Thanks, Opal. I appreciate your promptness. I've got a fantastic idea rolling around in my head right now. I'll be in touch soon."

While Perry and Reginald chatted about the up-keep of Stone Gate, Lorene nibbled on a tasty cookie and ate the sherbet, but her thoughts weren't on the food. Should she be so daring? Was she out of line to ask? Reginald wouldn't have to agree, and after all, he wanted a big celebration.

When Perry mentioned he had an appointment in an hour, they stood to leave, and Lorene said, "Mr. Peters, I'm going to suggest something, and if you don't want to do it, no hard feelings."

"Speak what's on your mind, Miss Harvey."

"As you know, the invitation to Jon Preston was a last-minute idea. He's agreed to come, but Woodston's accommodations have been booked for months. I hesitate to send them to Evansville for the short time they'll be here. We'll need housing for only ten people, and space to park several motor homes. Would you consider hosting Preston's entourage here at Stone Gate? It would be a wonderful experience for them to stay in a home like this."

Lorene could tell that he was intrigued by the idea, but Reginald hadn't lived eighty years without learning caution. "I'll have to think about it, but I'll give you my answer before noon tomorrow. Will that be soon enough?''

''Yes, and thanks for even considering it.''

''Do you think I was too bold in asking such a thing?'' Lorene asked Perry as they drove away from Stone Gate.

His laugh was low and rich. ''Not at all. That's the best possible solution to the situation. Let's face it—even if there were vacant rooms, Woodston's motel accommodations aren't luxurious.''

With a mischievous grin Lorene said, ''I know. That's the reason I'm living at Riverview Ridge. Do you think he'll do it?''

''Yes, I do. Kentucky Colonels are known for their generosity and promotion of the Commonwealth. He loves that estate, and he'll enjoy playing host to a celebrity. Let's pray that Mr. Preston will live up to his reputation.''

''It's too late to change our minds, but I wish I'd listened to one of Preston's recordings. I should have done that before I even agreed to promote Preston, but of course, hindsight is always twenty-twenty.''

Reginald telephoned the next morning soon after Lorene had returned from a brisk walk to the river.

''I'll host the Preston group, Miss Harvey, and pay all the expense, if—'' he paused, and she could sense a smile spreading across his wrinkled face

"—you'll make all the catering arrangements and serve as my hostess. If we're going to do this, I want to do it right."

How could she possibly add anything else to her already-heaped-up plate?

"What do you mean by catering arrangements?" she hedged.

"You take care of floral decorations, plan the meals, assign the rooms, see to table arrangements and stay at Stone Gate as my hostess while the guests are here. I'll provide the home and the money—everything else is up to you."

"Uh, let me give this some thought. First of all, I'll have to come back to your house and look over the accommodations closely, tally bath and room locations, and then find out if any of Preston's group can share rooms. I came up with this brainstorm on the spur of the moment, and I still think it's a good idea, but I'll have to see how it'll work out. May I come out again this afternoon and look around?"

"I may not be here, but I'll leave word that you're to have free run of the house and the estate. I appreciate the work you're doing for Woodston."

Lorene sent off an e-mail to Opal, explaining the possibility of using the Peters estate to entertain Jon Preston and his group, adding, "Please tell them what kind of home they'd be staying in, and see if they agree. Also, try to figure out the number of single rooms and double rooms required, and the time of their arrival and departure from Woodston.

If they won't stay at Stone Gate, there's no possibility except to house them at Evansville, and that's a long drive from Woodston. Thanks.''

She hustled downstairs to tell Dottie of the newest development and asked if she could call an impromptu meeting in her dining room that evening. "I'll see if Perry can come, and you and John can sit in with us."

"If you'll meet at seven, the other guests will have eaten by then, and we can have the dining room to ourselves."

"Good. I want to talk privately, so the whole town won't know where Preston is staying until we've got all the details nailed down."

"Gotcha," Dottie said. "But the news will leak out anyway."

Chapter Eleven

Two of Dottie's customers were still eating when Lorene and Perry entered the dining room. Dottie waved them to a table and brought iced glasses of fruit punch.

"It won't be long," she said in an undertone. "Relax a while and enjoy your beverage. That punch is made from a secret recipe. It'll give you an appetite."

Perry reached for Lorene's hand, and his eyes swept over her features in concern.

"You look exhausted. The commission has expected too much of you." He lowered his voice. "Or is it emotional fallout?"

She curled her fingers to wrap around his, and he tightened his grip. "Oh, I don't know, Perry. A little of both, I suppose. I'm not sleeping well. For one thing, I dread to have Dad show up in Woodston again. He's not above accosting you in public, and I don't want to be the cause of ruining your reputation at the college. Alma's indicated the faculty has to live above reproach."

"Let me worry about that. It won't be your fault."

"It will be if my own father spreads gossip about you."

"I haven't had any black marks against my character during the years I've lived in Woodston, and I don't believe the college board will censure me for something that happened twenty years ago. If I'm not worrying, you don't have to, either."

He chucked her under the chin. "I'd like to see that wide smile of yours and the little crinkles that highlight your eyes when you're happy. Come on, smile great big," he said in the tone he would use to a child. "Pretty please."

Lorene felt a warm glow in her heart, and a slight smile tipped the corners of her mouth. As it widened, the muscles of her face relaxed.

"That's better," Perry said quietly.

"No one can be happy and bubbly all the time."

"Yes, I know that, but I don't want you to be unhappy because of me."

They were reminded they weren't alone when Dottie approached the table and placed napkins and silverware before them. "Not much longer now," she whispered.

When the last customers finished dessert and left,

Dottie locked the door. John came from the kitchen carrying a tray of grilled chicken breasts, baked potatoes, green beans and hot rolls. Dottie placed small bowls of melon balls and mixed fruit beside each place setting. She surveyed the table. "Okay, that's everything. Let's eat before we start planning. I'm hungry."

After they finished the meal, the Montgomerys cleared away the dishes and Dottie brought chilled dishes of orange sorbet for dessert.

"We can eat sorbet and talk at the same time, can't we?" Lorene said. "I called this private meeting because we'll need to keep quiet about our plans to house Preston at Stone Gate until he agrees to it, but I must make some preliminary plans."

"I can't imagine anyone turning down a chance to stay at that mansion," Dottie said.

"Stone Gate probably doesn't mean a thing to anyone except this county's residents," Perry mentioned.

"Let's brainstorm a little," Lorene said as she nibbled on a wafer stuck into the sorbet. "Reginald's employees can furnish home-cooked meals for Preston's staff. But I think we should have a reception after the concert, probably on the lawn, for a large group of Woodston residents, and perhaps a dinner for Preston and his family with only a few local people invited to it. I'll check when I go to Stone Gate tomorrow to see how many people can be seated in the dining room. The dinner and reception will have to be catered. Is there a catering service in Woodston?''

''The family restaurant on Main Street could probably handle that,'' John said. ''They do weddings and anniversaries, and their food is good. I imagine they can provide for one or two hundred guests.''

''Who'd be invited to the reception?'' Perry asked.

Lorene shook her head. ''The commission members will have to come up with a list. That's the reason I wanted your input. You'll know who's been a big help in planning and pulling off this celebration.''

''We should invite the ones who've donated money for promotion, as well as the merchants who've done some personal advertising,'' Dottie suggested.

''Perhaps the artisans who take part in the flatboat arrival and stay at the fort during the week?'' Perry wondered.

''How many would that total?''

''Anywhere between eighty and a hundred guests, I'd think,'' Dottie said.

''Let's make a list,'' Perry suggested, ''and then have Mr. Kincaid and Reginald okay it.''

''I'd prefer to have the reception outdoors, although if the weather is bad, the house is roomy enough that we could move inside,'' Lorene said.

''Lorene, are you sure you can take this on in

addition to everything else you have to do?'' Perry said, still concerned about her.

She smiled her thanks at him. "Since I asked Reginald to host Preston's group, I don't have much choice. I'll be okay. Besides, it's all part of my job.''

Both Perry and the Montgomerys offered advice to make Lorene's work easier, and before the evening was over she'd learned which florist was the most capable, where to rent linens and towels if Stone Gate's supplies weren't enough, and where to look for musicians who could provide a nineteenth-century musical background for the dinner. She wanted someone to play the harpsichord owned by Reginald, and a violinist and a cellist to make up a string trio.

When the Montgomerys went to the kitchen to finish their work for the night, Perry and Lorene drifted to the back porch.

"Do you have work to do tonight, or is it all right for me to come to your apartment for a while?''

"I always have work to do,'' she answered, "but I'm never too busy for you.''

His hand on her arm was tender and yet protective as they turned toward the stairs. Lorene laid aside her notes when they entered the living room.

"Let's sit on the balcony. I haven't had the air conditioner on today, and it's stuffy in here. There's one chair out there, and we can take another one from the kitchen.''

Following her with a chair in his hand, Perry said, "I didn't know there was a balcony."

"Actually," Lorene said, humor in her voice, "it's a fire escape, but the upper ledge is wide enough for me to sit and meditate while I have my morning coffee."

There was hardly room for two chairs, but they placed them close together, and Perry put his arm over her shoulders. He exclaimed over the view of the river, still faintly visible in the dusk from their high vantage point. "This is a great retreat! And private, too."

Dusk hovered over the valley, and the lights of a towboat churning upriver gleamed in the distance. They heard the steady hum of the diesel engines over the droning of a few katydids and other autumn insects in the trees. A pleasant breeze floated by them, riffling Lorene's long hair and blowing it across Perry's face. He grasped the soft tendrils and lifted them to his lips.

Lorene had done so much talking in the conference that she was glad Perry didn't need to be entertained. It was satisfying to sit close, their bodies touching, feeling the light weight of his arm on her shoulders.

Perry thought, but didn't say, that this quiet interlude brought out vividly the contentment they'd missed during the years they'd been separated.

God, You've given us a second chance. Help us

not to mess up. How can I keep from losing her this time?

Perry sighed deeply, and Lorene lifted a hand and touched his face. "It's nice to be together and not have to say anything, isn't it? Wonderful that we can enjoy the whispers of our hearts."

"Yes," he said, and moved his head to nibble her fingers. "We haven't lost our knack of communicating without words." He sighed again. "But it's time for me to go."

In the darkness he searched for her lips and found them. His kiss was sweet and warm—a kiss that brought comfort to the weary places of her soul and body. The flame that had been kindled between them the first time they'd pledged their love had smoldered during their long separation, but it was blazing again.

"Good night, Lorene," he said huskily, then pulled her up and held her momentarily in a snug embrace. He inhaled the spicy fragrance of her perfume.

Whispering against his lips, she said, "Thanks for spending this quiet time with me. I haven't been so relaxed for weeks. I'll sleep well tonight."

The visit to Stone Gate supplied Lorene with the other information she needed. Several rooms provided bed space for twelve people, but according to Reginald's housekeeper, Mrs. Cossin, there weren't enough bed linens and towels to take care of so many guests. Lorene made a note that these, too, must be rented. It was still a week before Preston would stay at Stone Gate, but she'd be busy all next week with the celebration, so she had to do as much as possible today.

With the housekeeper's help, Lorene tallied the china, silver and glassware available in the house and checked the size of the dining-room table. Mrs. Cossin was a diminutive woman, probably in her fifties, and she and her husband had been employed at Stone Gate for twenty years.

"Mr. Peters is an odd man in many ways," she said, "though he's a good employer. But 'deed I don't see how we'll manage to take care of such a big bunch of people. He has dinner guests two or three times a year, and he nearly worries me to death then, changing his mind and all."

Lorene laughed good-naturedly. "I've experienced his mind-changing, and Mr. Kincaid's, too, but Mr. Peters asked me to make all the plans for entertaining Jon Preston and his entourage. Since he left all the details up to me, once you and I have agreed on everything, I won't change my mind."

Mrs. Cossin shook her head uncertainly. "Let's hope he sticks to that."

"I'll insist that he does. That's a little easier for me to do than for you, when you have to see him every day. If he and I disagree, which we're likely to do, as soon as Heritage Week is over, I'll be gone, and I won't have to live with his displeasure."

"Men *are* odd creatures, ain't they?" Mrs. Cossin mentioned. "But I'll get along all right with you. Just tell me what you want done, and I'll do it."

Lorene shook hands with her.

"I'll probably be in and out of the house so much you'll get tired of seeing me. I'll make my plans and talk them over with Mr. Peters to get his approval before I pass along your duties. Right now everything hinges on Jon Preston's response. Thanks so much."

A message from her office was on Lorene's computer when she returned.

"Preston agrees to stay at Stone Gate," Opal had written. "Telephone me, and we'll discuss the details."

Her phone was in her hand before she finished reading the e-mail.

"That was fast work," she said approvingly when Opal answered. "Thanks. My hands were tied on that part of the project until we learned Preston's wishes."

"As I told you earlier, most of his technical crew travel in RVs and live in them on the site. I don't know how old Preston is, but he isn't married, and his parents travel with him. There's one other couple. The way I figure it, the two married couples can occupy two rooms, and Preston can have a private. The five single men can double up without any problem. Think you can swing that?"

"No trouble at all. I'll be staying in the house,

too, but it's a small room off the kitchen. That would still leave an extra room if we need it."

"We've been receiving lots of applications for new work. Do you want me to tell you about them now?"

"Oh, I don't think so," Lorene said warily. "Unless there's something that calls for an immediate decision. This celebration demands my full concentration. I'll need a day or two to wrap up everything, but I should be back in Pittsburgh within two weeks. Take care of everything the best you can until then."

Two more weeks and she'd be leaving Perry! Could she really tear herself away from him again after six weeks of seeing and talking to him every day? Her mind returned to the present when Opal said, "Oh, by the way, Preston will arrive Saturday afternoon, but he doesn't want anybody bothering him. He likes to check out the performance area and do some practicing ahead of time, then spend the night relaxing. The concert is scheduled for two o'clock on Sunday. He'll stay at Stone Gate until after the reception and dinner, then travel overnight to Nashville, where he has a recording date on Monday morning. How does that schedule sound?"

"We can work around it. I don't know how much relaxing he'll have Saturday night. Mr. Kincaid has booked Preston's party for an evening cruise on the *River Queen*, a replica of a nineteenth-century steamer."

"Sounds romantic. Are you going?"

"Nope. I'm down here to work, not socialize. Be sure to keep check on those TV advertisements to see that they air on schedule. I don't have time to watch television."

Since Lorene intended to spend Heritage Week camping at the fort, she ordered two more frontier costumes from the rental place in Louisville. They were more elaborate than the dress Dottie had made for her.

"I doubt that the pioneers had such fancy clothes," she said to Perry and Alma when she stopped by his office to find out what else she needed to camp at the fort.

"I'm sure the founders of Fort Woodston didn't own more than one dress at a time," Perry teased her. "I'll have to make do with one outfit," he continued. "My Daniel Boone costume was quite expensive—one's all I can afford. And I don't intend to shave for a week, either," he warned.

"Lots of men will be unshaven," Alma said. "Besides, it might be good for Lorene to see how scruffy you can look sometimes."

Lorene's face flushed when she realized that Alma was still matchmaking. Pushing her hair back from her forehead to cover her confusion, Lorene said, "I don't expect camping at the fort to be much fun. I've committed to stay there through Thursday, then I want to move to Stone Gate and be settled in by Saturday morning to help Mrs. Cossin and the other workers put the finishing touches on the house.''

Perry walked down the hallway with her. ''Don't pay any attention to Alma's teasing,'' he said. ''I just ignore her hints.''

''It would be better if my face wasn't an open book every time I look at you, Perry, but I'm not a very good actress.''

He put both hands on her shoulders. ''Your face might be an open book, but it must be written in a foreign language. Most of the time I can't read what it says.'' His eyes searched her unreadable features, and his touch was electrifying.

His nearness overwhelmed her, and, swallowing with difficulty, she murmured, ''If you'd read between the lines, you'd probably learn that I want you to kiss me.''

Perry didn't even spare a glance to see if anyone was watching. His hands slid down her back and he gathered her into his arms. Her knees weakened and her senses reeled, for his kiss was as rewarding and welcome as a whisper to her heart.

Chapter Twelve

When Lorene's alarm clock sounded on the last Saturday in September, she thanked God that the sun was shining. After all the town's preparation, it would have been disappointing to start the celebration with a rain-drenched parade. The weather was something Lorene couldn't control, but while she ate breakfast she checked the weather channel. The dry forecast called for above-normal temperatures during the next ten days, which was welcome news.

Mr. Kincaid had insisted that Lorene must ride on the bicentennial commission's float, following the color guard in the parade. Deciding to save Dottie's comfortable creation for living at the fort, Lorene chose one of the dresses she'd rented, a pale lavender gown made of fabric that resembled the homespun linsey-woolsey woven by pioneer women out of linen and wool. She wore two petticoats and a white smock apron over the dress with a sunbonnet of matching fabric.

The parade was scheduled to begin at nine o'clock, and since the temperature was already seventy degrees when Lorene got out of bed, she knew she would long for shorts, rather than pioneer garments, before the week was over. When Lorene joined the others at the beginning of the parade route, Alma, dressed as a rich matron rather than a lowly pioneer, ambled over to her, holding up her skirts a few inches, with a resigned expression on her face.

"I don't know about you, but I'm going to shed these petticoats when we move out to the fort. I'm about to roast. How did the pioneers stand it?"

"We're softer than our ancestors were," Lorene answered, laughter in her voice. "They'd never heard of shorts, slacks or air-conditioning."

"Chalk that up as another reason I'm happy I live in this century," Alma said.

Zeb Denney, in his police uniform rather than costume, helped Alma and Lorene board the flatbed truck, decorated with red, white and blue bunting. Miniature Kentucky flags hung from benches where the commission members and guests were to sit.

"I figured I'd better be wearing my pistol instead of carrying a bow and arrow or a muzzle-loading gun," he said, "in case we run into any trouble today."

"Are you expecting trouble?" Lorene asked anxiously. After all her hard work, she didn't want any demonstrations or riots.

"Naw!" Zeb assured her. "The crowd is peaceful, but it never hurts to have a cop or two in sight."

Reginald Peters's costume had been copied from a portrait of his ancestor who'd been one of the first settlers in western Kentucky. Mr. Kincaid was dressed as a circuit-riding preacher. When Perry joined them, wearing his deerskin garment and coonskin cap, they did make a festive-looking group, and Lorene was happy to be a part of it. Perry's beard had been growing for a week, and he rubbed it when he sat beside Lorene.

"What do you think of my whiskers?"

"They look like a cross between a briar patch and a scouring pad. You'd make a good Santa."

"Hey, you really know how to hurt a guy! I thought I looked distinguished."

Glancing around to see if anyone was listening, Lorene lowered her voice. "You always look good to me, but, as far as I'm concerned, the mustache is enough for me."

Before Perry could answer, the signal was given for the parade to start, and when the commission members took their places, there was no more time for intimate conversation.

Lorene had hired two photographers to cover the event, and as the parade got under way, she saw they were in place. She'd made arrangements for the opening festivities of Heritage Week to be shown on the evening news in Kentucky and all the bordering states. She already had many tour groups committed to attend, but she still hoped to lure the undecided to help Woodston celebrate. She saw vans from television stations in Evansville and Louisville, experiencing a sense of satisfaction that she'd been able to accomplish so much in a short amount of time.

The parade wound down Main Street for about a mile, and both sides of the street were lined with spectators. Numerous 4-H clubs had prepared floats, and since it was an election year, several politicians rode along, as well. Two school bands played military and patriotic music. Not a large parade, but one typical of Woodston, and that's what the people wanted.

The weather was perfect for September—temperature in the low eighties, a sunny sky and a cool breeze. Lorene couldn't have asked for better results.

During the general dispersion at the end of the parade, Perry drew Lorene to one side.

"I've bought two tickets for Saturday's moonlight cruise on the *River Queen*. Will you go with me?"

She wanted very much to go, for as the clock ticked toward the end of the bicentennial, it was on her mind constantly that in a few days she would leave Woodston, which meant leaving Perry, too.

"I'll be at Stone Gate Saturday night, looking after Jon Preston and his personnel."

Perry shook his head, and the coon's tail on his

cap dangled over his shoulder. "They're going on the cruise, too, so they won't be at Stone Gate for you to entertain." Oblivious to the crowd around them, he took her hand, his dark eyes brimming with tenderness and eagerness. "I really want you to go with me."

She hesitated, shuffling her feet.

"Don't you want to go?" Perry persisted.

She lifted confused, wistful eyes. "I want to be with you whatever we do. I keep remembering that in a few more days we'll be separated again."

"Then let's take advantage of every minute we can find to be together."

"Thanks, Perry. I'd love to go with you on the cruise." But she added, her eyes bright with merriment, "I'll go, but only if you've shaved."

"The whiskers will come off Saturday morning," he promised, "but I was hoping to kiss you once before I shaved, just to scratch your face."

"No way," she teased.

"Did you know that Mr. Peters has invited me to spend the weekend at Stone Gate? He says there's an extra room. Will that upset your sleeping arrangements?"

"Not at all. There *is* an extra room if someone doesn't show up unexpectedly. If Preston brings another bodyguard or musician that I hadn't counted on, I'll let you know."

After Lorene left him and started homeward, her thoughts were momentarily diverted from the celebration to wonder what she'd wear on Saturday night. She contemplated going to Evansville and buying a new dress, but she didn't have time for that. She'd have to rely on what she'd brought from Pittsburgh.

Although Lorene had been hoping they wouldn't, her parents returned on Sunday afternoon while she was making final plans to move to the fort. They still hadn't found a room for the week, so Lorene said, "I won't be sleeping at the apartment all week. You can use my bedroom. I'm camping at the fort for a few days, and then I'll be at Stone Gate over the weekend."

"We'd hoped to spend some time with you," Celeste complained.

"Then you chose a poor time to visit me," Lorene answered lightly, trying to stifle the anger she still felt toward her father for the way he'd treated Perry. "I won't have any free time all week."

"Then we might as well go home," Addison said, and Lorene wished they would leave, but she doubted that would happen.

"We'll stay for a few days," Celeste said.

"Then feel free to use the apartment. I'll be here off and on, but not overnight."

"What's this camping at the fort involve?" Addison demanded.

"Quite a few visiting artisans and some local people are going to spend the week instructing guests about the history of Woodston.''

''Now that I'm over my anger,'' Addison said harshly, and Lorene doubted that he'd stopped being angry, ''I want to have a talk with you about Perry Saunders. I hope you don't get involved with him again.''

Praying for patience, Lorene said, ''Having reached the age of forty, if I'm not able to make my own decisions, I never will be. Are you ever going to let me live my own life?''

''Are you taking up with Saunders again?'' her father insisted.

''I'm thinking about it. The worst mistake I ever made was letting you convince me that Perry no longer wanted me. We've missed twenty years of happiness, as well as losing our son, because you weren't honest with me.''

''Don't ever mention that to me again,'' Addison shouted.

''The day you took my baby away from me,'' Lorene continued doggedly, ''was the day I decided you'd never rule my life any longer.''

Celeste was crying softly. ''Addison, please.''

''If you marry him, I'll cut you off without a penny.''

''Good! I don't need your money, and I think that's what rankles you most of all. I don't have to turn to you for support like I did when my baby needed a home. And as for Perry, I don't know if we have any future together, but we'll make that decision, not you.''

"If you marry him, you'll never be welcome at my home."

"I'm sorry you feel that way, but if I have another opportunity for happiness with Perry, I'm taking it."

"Come on, Celeste, we're leaving."

"Please, Addison, I want to stay for Heritage Week."

"No," he said bluntly, and walked out of the apartment without a backward look.

Lorene put her arms around Celeste's shaking shoulders.

"I wish you wouldn't anger your father, Lorene. He's impossible to live with when he's angry at one of his daughters. I want you to be able to come home."

"This isn't the first time Dad has threatened to kick me out. He'll get over it. He'd never pass up the opportunity to interfere in my life."

"Well, I'll have to leave, but I don't want to. Lorene, I've always been sorry that we didn't keep the baby. I've wondered about him so many times."

"Me, too," Lorene whispered, and she held tightly to her mother's hand. "I figure Dad has also, and that's one thing that makes him so cantankerous. The only grandson he had to carry on the family line, and he wouldn't accept him. Take care of yourself, Mother. I'll keep in touch with you."

Tearfully Celeste followed her husband, giving in

to his domination as she always had. Lorene wondered if all of their lives wouldn't have been better if Celeste had mustered the courage to oppose her husband.

The episode didn't disturb Lorene a great deal, for she'd been through many similar incidents with her father since she'd gone out on her own. He was always advising her about her investments, about how to run the company, which car to buy and which one not to. Through the years she'd grown a thick veneer against his interference, and she paid little attention to him. But where Perry was concerned, she'd always been vulnerable, and his verbal attack on Perry was something she wouldn't tolerate. If they'd stayed in town, she would have been edgy all week, wondering what her father might say or do to embarrass Perry. Having her parents around was more trauma than she wanted to deal with during the celebration. It was a relief to hear their car drive away.

Activities at the fort were scheduled to begin at nine o'clock on Monday morning with the arrival of the two rafts, loaded with almost thirty people. On Sunday afternoon John Montgomery and Zeb took the flatboats upstream, two miles from the Denney place, and anchored them at a pleasure-craft landing dock. The two men slept on the flatboats to forestall any vandalism.

Since Lorene intended to go to the apartment each

day to check on her mail, she didn't take many personal items to the fort. She and Alma had coordinated their packing so they wouldn't duplicate any essentials. She'd loaded the station wagon on Sunday afternoon and moved enough items into their cabin at the fort to assure a minimum of comfort during the week.

Participants in the flatboat journey had been admonished to arrive no later than eight o'clock, which was no problem for Lorene. The biggest nuisance was driving her station wagon in the long skirt, so she left her vehicle at the fort on Sunday evening, and Perry picked her up at the apartment before half-past seven. They were at the landing in plenty of time.

Lorene's photographers were on hand, interviewing the make-believe pioneers, and she also saw two men from the major networks. So far she hadn't been disappointed by any of the media who'd promised to cover the bicentennial.

John bellowed out instructions when he got everyone on board. "I don't want to spoil the authenticity of our little river jaunt by wearing life preservers, but I want every one of you to have your hand on a life jacket as we float along. I don't expect any trouble, but we have to be prepared."

When the flatboats cast off, Dottie started singing "Beautiful Ohio," a song Lorene had often heard in Pittsburgh, where the Ohio River began.

Maple trees, sycamores and willows grew along

the river, and as the flatboats hugged the bank, the occupants had to dodge an occasional tree branch overhanging the water.

Canada geese and ducks lifted gracefully into flight when the boats glided by their feeding areas.

An occasional carp flipped out of the water, its wet silver body gleaming in the sunlight.

Sun rays soon disintegrated the few pockets of fog.

If it hadn't been for the soft purr of the motor that kept them on course, Lorene could easily have felt transported into a former century. The flatboats glided smoothly, and the tranquil setting filled Lorene's soul with serenity and turned her thoughts toward God.

After Perry had poled the raft for a while, he sat beside her. "'Be still and know that I am God,'" she quoted softly, and he nodded with understanding.

The other passengers were otherwise occupied, and for a moment it was as if she and Perry were alone.

"I've been thinking the same thing," he said, and although he didn't touch her, the light smoldering in his eyes thrilled Lorene as much as an intimate caress. "No matter what the future brings," he murmured, "I'm happy we can share this experience. It wouldn't have been the same without you."

"Thanks for telling me," she whispered just as

Dottie turned toward them, destroying their tranquil moment.

"This is kinda fun," Dottie said. "Pioneers didn't have it so bad."

"I don't know about that," Lorene said hesitantly. "What did they do when there was a downpour? Where would they have taken a bath or found privacy for other personal functions? And there was no place to hide if Indians started shooting arrows at them. I think two miles is as far as I'd want to ride on a flatboat."

"Spoilsport!" Dottie accused with a laugh.

A large crowd waited at the fort, and they cheered when the flatboats came into view. Their arrival suffered a temporary setback when one exuberant poler dipped too deeply into the river and lost his balance. Without the help of two of his companions, he would have ended up in the water. And the mosquitoes were a little too friendly to suit Lorene, but she counted the trip a success. She especially enjoyed it because it wasn't one of her responsibilities.

They walked inside the fort, where Mr. Kincaid was acting as a guide to several state officials who'd come to take part in dedicating the fort. A rail fence circled the stockade. Although on a smaller scale, the fort was built very much like the original structure might have been. There were blockhouses at each corner, complete with gun ports. Small cabins, built around the inside wall, were windowless rooms with dirt floors. Cabin furnishings were limited to a table and a few chairs. Wooden frames attached to the walls, laced with ropes to support thin cornhusk mattresses, served as beds.

"I wouldn't have had the stamina to be a pioneer woman," Lorene said to Perry as she looked at the room she'd occupy for the next few nights.

"It would have been a hard life. Back then no one had luxuries like we do in this century. But you'd have been a success at being a pioneer wife if you'd lived then."

A satisfied expression glowed in her eyes when she noticed how the buckskin outfit emphasized Perry's beautifully proportioned physique, and she said pointedly, "Maybe—if I'd had a strong man to lean on."

"You'd have made the right choice in that direction, too. I have a lot of confidence in you."

"You always had more confidence in me than I had in myself," she commented, recalling how often Perry had encouraged her in college when she thought she couldn't complete an assignment.

His dark eyes were gentle and understanding, and words of endearment trembled on his lips. Mr. Kincaid approached to introduce his distinguished guests, and their retreat into nostalgia flittered away.

Before noon, the fort area was overrun with schoolchildren, and Perry and Lorene walked around the large parking area checking bus and automobile licenses, noting that there were visitors from all the neighboring states—Missouri, Illinois, Indiana,

Ohio, West Virginia, Virginia and Tennessee. The
trend continued through the week as tourists of all
ages swarmed through downtown Woodston buying
souvenirs and loitering at the fort to watch demonstrations of log splitting, cornhusking and grinding,
candle making and other crafts.

Since Lorene didn't have any artisan talents, she'd
been designated the cook for herself, Perry and the
Denneys. Over a campfire she heated soups and
stews that Dottie and John had prepared in advance.
Although it looked authentic, actually she was only
warming up the already cooked food. She had a
small skillet, an iron pot and coffeepot to set on a
portable grill to prepare their breakfast. In spite of
the help from modern conveniences, after her first
day as cook Lorene had a keener appreciation of the
vicissitudes of pioneer living. And occasionally she
lapsed into daydreams of how she and Perry might
have fared as man and wife on the frontier.

Chapter Thirteen

Living in the fort didn't prove too unpleasant for the campers. It wasn't an experience that Lorene would have wanted to undergo permanently, but she did enjoy the camaraderie of those who depicted the past, and the wide-eyed wonder of children as they viewed the work of artisans from a bygone era.

The room Alma and Lorene shared had no window, and as she stumbled around Monday night getting ready for bed by the light of one small candle, Lorene said, "I had no idea how dark it would be."

A fire burning in the middle of the stockade provided a little light, for only a canvas covered the opening to their cabin. Perry and Zeb had bedded down in sleeping bags in front of the door, so neither of the women was concerned about prowlers.

"I know," Alma said. "We used to go camping

when our boy was little, but I haven't been in complete darkness since then.''

"I have a feeling this is going to get old before Friday."

"Wait until you try out your bed," Alma said, giggling.

When Lorene lay down on her cot, the ropes sagged almost to the dirt floor.

Perry heard Alma and Lorene laughing, and he called, "What's the matter? Are you having trouble adjusting to the rigors of frontier living?"

"These beds are terrible. We won't be able to sleep at all," Alma answered.

"Did you ever try a sleeping bag on the hard ground?" Perry asked.

"Not for a long time," Alma answered.

"Well, it's not luxury, either," Zeb grunted. "Stop giggling and go to sleep—remember, frontier women were submissive to their husbands."

"Yeah, I remember that. Another reason I'm glad I live in the twenty-first century," Alma retorted.

But with Perry sleeping nearby, at that moment Lorene could think of worse things than submitting to one's husband.

The capabilities of the local artisans surprised Lorene. Having hired extra helpers to operate the B and B, Dottie spent several hours at the fort each day spinning raw wool into thread. Alma and another woman hand-dipped candles. Lorene felt rather useless, but she encouraged the artisans by bringing them refreshments and running errands for them.

When she complained of her ineptness to Perry, he whispered, "We need a touch of beauty around here, and you're taking care of that. Do you know you're even prettier now than you were when I first met you?"

"I appreciate those kind remarks, but I doubt they're completely true." She favored him with a pert, captivating smile, but her heart fluttered at the enjoyment in his eyes when he looked at her.

After the gates to the park closed to visitors on Wednesday night, Mr. Kincaid called a brief meeting of commission members to assess the week's activities. His beaming face indicated that the celebration was proceeding to his satisfaction.

"We've averaged more than four thousand people every day at the fort, and the business owners in town say that business has been good."

"And I think we owe most of that to Miss Harvey, our PR lady," Reginald Peters said, clapping his hands. "You've done a good job for us. Although at first I thought the price for your services was high, it's obvious that you're worth every penny of it."

"Thanks," Lorene responded. "I was afraid I couldn't arrange what you wanted, since I got in on the job rather late, but the response has been better than I expected. And my Pittsburgh office manager reports that the Preston concert is sold out.''

Rubbing his hands together in satisfaction, Mr. Kincaid said, ''Yes, indeed—we've even put Woodston on the international map! Two busloads of Asian tourists came yesterday.''

Her experiences at the fort furnished Lorene with a better understanding of pioneer life and a greater appreciation of what hardships they endured. She felt guilty each day when she took off a few hours to go to the apartment to wash her hair, shower and change clothing—none of which the pioneers could have done. Then she sat at the best electronic equipment available to conduct business in Pittsburgh in a matter of seconds. In Woodston's beginning, the pioneers would have been completely cut off from the rest of the world. So she was also gaining a new appreciation of the blessings of modern conveniences.

Thursday night, after the fort's residents enjoyed a catered evening meal, they pulled benches around the campfire. As they discussed the week's events, Lorene tried to share some of her thoughts with the others. ''It's been a time of revelation for me,'' she said. ''I've never really appreciated my heritage before. My father's ancestors lived in Kentucky, so I feel as if I have some roots here, too. The things I've learned this week make me proud of my ancestry.''

Each night, Perry had held a short devotional before they went to bed, reciting Scripture from memory. Now, in the faint light from the embers of the fire, he pointed upward.

"This week we've blundered around in the darkness preparing for bed, sometimes complaining about the lack of light, but we've been earthbound, not looking in the right direction."

His listeners followed his sweeping hand, and as one, they gave an exclamation of awe. Above them, a myriad of stars beautified the night, and a brilliant half-moon hung above them on the eastern side of the fort.

"'The heavens declare the glory of God; the skies proclaim the work of His hands,'" Perry quoted from the nineteenth psalm. "When we lose our way, it's well for us to look to the heavens for guidance as the pioneers did.

"These few days of plain living may have taught us a greater lesson than any instruction we've passed on to the schoolchildren. Our ancestors depended upon God for all their needs because they were cut off from family and friends. They had a harsh way of living, as we've learned this week, and yet they were strengthened by God."

He paused for a few moments to allow everyone to contemplate the impact the week's activities had had on them personally.

"God," he prayed, "help us to become worthy stewards of the spiritual torch our ancestors have passed to us."

Perry and Lorene remained by the fire after the others retired for the night, careful to keep at a discreet distance. Even though they'd been together all week, they'd been under the eyes of the public, so they had kept their outward emotions in check, but tonight Perry had asked her to stay behind. His thoughts were troubled, and he needed assurance from her.

Talking quietly so that those in the cabins and tents couldn't hear him, he said, "I've been proud of you all week. You've done a tremendous job with this celebration. I had no idea how skilled you are in your profession."

His words filled her with a warm glow. "You had a hand in it, you know. If you hadn't encouraged me to go into another field when it was so obvious I wasn't cut out to be an engineer, I might have left college."

"But it troubles me, too. When you're so good at what you're doing, I wonder if there is any future for us. When I mentioned that we should get married, you didn't seem too taken with the idea."

"But I've been thinking about it," she hastened to assure him. "I could set up my agency's headquarters in any large city, because much of my business comes from all over the country. Evansville or Louisville would be large enough."

"But you travel a lot, and I can't ask you to change your business practices. Perhaps marrying me is a sacrifice I shouldn't ask you to make."

Even in the dim light he could see the laughter in her eyes. "Are you trying to hedge on your proposal?"

"You know better! This week has been sheer torture to me—you've been so near, but yet so far from where I want you to be."

She touched her lips and wafted a kiss to him through the smoke that spiraled upward between them. "When the time comes, the way will be plain for us. We'll know what's right to do."

"I'm praying that God will give us the answer."

"Then He will—just keep praying. Somehow I feel that once we've put Heritage Week behind us, we'll know what decisions to make," Lorene concluded, still concerned that he hadn't mentioned loving her. He'd told her the day he found out about their son that he'd thought nothing she could do would stop him from loving her. If she remembered correctly, he hadn't mentioned loving or forgiving her since that time. As much as she wanted to take her place by Perry's side, she wouldn't consider a marriage without love.

"When are you going to Stone Gate?" he asked.

"Tomorrow afternoon. Reginald's household staff are excited and very nervous about entertaining a celebrity. The caterers are going to set up their tents tomorrow. I need to be there to advise them, but I'll have my phone nearby all the time if you need me. And I'll be at your office Saturday morning when the Louisville station broadcasts a live interview of the bicentennial commission's take on the celebration.''

After the other centennial commission members left his office Saturday morning, Perry stood behind Lorene's chair and massaged her neck to relieve the tension.

"That helps," she said. "I'm usually not so keyed up over a project, but this one has had too many emotional distractions."

"Am I an emotional distraction?" he teased.

"You always have been, but I wouldn't have it any other way."

Rapid footsteps approached, and when two young men entered the office, Perry assumed they were potential students. "I'm Perry Saunders," he said. "Come in."

The visitors were both healthy specimens of manhood, and Lorene's heartbeat stopped for one poignant moment when they entered. One man was of medium height and slender, with neat, shoulder-length dark hair and serious gray eyes. His movements were quick, full of purpose and vitality.

His companion had a tall, athletic build. A lock of unruly coal-black hair hung over his forehead, and a glimmering smile starting in his jet-black eyes spread to lips that were firm and generous. Broad, muscular shoulders strained against the fabric of his white shirt, contrasting sharply with his narrow waist and hips. He walked with a swinging, long-legged stride.

Perry stepped forward as the slender man glanced expectantly around the room. "I'm Jon Preston. We arrived in town earlier than we expected. I was told the bicentennial commission was meeting here, so I thought I'd come in and introduce myself."

"It's a pleasure to meet you," Perry said. "The meeting has already adjourned, but I'm a member of the commission. Let me be the first to welcome you to Woodston, Mr. Preston."

"Please call me Jon," he said, taking Perry's hand in a warm grasp. "When someone says Mr. Preston, I think they're talking about my father," he added with a smile.

"Very well, Jon," Perry conceded. Perry laid a hand on Lorene's shoulder, and she welcomed the steadying influence of his tender touch, wondering if he could detect her inward tremors. "This is Lorene Harvey of Tri-State Public Relations, the agency that's handling advertising for your appearance."

"Glad to meet you, Miss Harvey," Jon said. "My dad arranged the details of the concert with your firm."

"And we're happy you could work Woodston into your schedule," she said, struggling to retain her equanimity and speak in a normal voice. "Everyone is excited about your appearance," she added with an effort, willing her eyes not to stray to Preston's companion.

"I'm a small-town boy, and it's a welcome break for us to come to a rural area," Jon said. "Oh, let me introduce my friend and, presently, my chauffeur and bodyguard, Chad Reece."

Lorene was still trembling when she extended her hand to Preston's friend.

"Mr. Reece looks as if he could give you all the protection you need," she said, her eyes admiring the way Chad's massive shoulders, muscular arms and slim hips molded into his red knit shirt and white shorts.

"I'm actually as tame as a kitten," Chad said in a gentle, laughing voice, "but I try to look ferocious when I think Jon needs protection."

"Gentle like a lion, maybe," Jon jeered. "Tell that to the players who oppose him every weekend during the football season. Chad plays for Wallace University's Golden Eagles in Alabama. He's recuperating from a slight injury, and he's had to take a few weeks off."

"So Jon took pity on me and gave me a job," Chad said, looking as if he needed no one's pity. "But I've had enough inactivity. I'll start practice next week."

"The rest of our group won't be along for a few hours," Jon said, "but I like to arrive incognito before the general public knows I'm here. I haven't gotten used to popularity yet." He laid a hand on

Chad's shoulder. "Chad's been a football hero since high school, and he's on his way to playing with the big guys. He thrives on applause, but I'm still shy."

"You can go to Stone Gate when you're ready, but would you like to look over the stadium before you're stampeded with fans?" Lorene asked.

"That sounds great," Jon said. "I suppose my technicians are on the job."

"They arrived yesterday and have been working this morning. The stadium has been closed, and no unauthorized persons will be allowed to enter until an hour before your concert."

"Sounds like you have everything under control. We'll have a short practice tomorrow morning to be sure everything works as it should."

"Perry and I have a few more things to discuss, and then I can devote the rest of the day to you."

"Super," Jon said. "That'll give us time to eat the breakfast we picked up at the drive-in east of town. Our van is parked beside the fountain. Come out when you're ready."

"Nice kids," Perry said as the two men exited the office.

Fixing him with a stare, Lorene asked, "Is that all you have to say?" She lifted a billfold from her purse, took out a picture and handed it to him. The image of Chad Reece in football uniform looked back at Perry, but it wasn't Chad's image. It was his own picture taken when he was a senior in high school, one he'd given Lorene soon after they'd met.

He stared at the picture for a few seconds and handed it back without meeting her eyes. "I hoped you wouldn't notice," he said softly.

"Not notice! I told you I've always believed I'd recognize our child on sight. When he walked into the room, I experienced a shock as powerful as a cosmic ray! My heart felt relieved, because I'd finally had the opportunity to see him again. But it was painful to think about how much I've missed by not seeing him grow up into such a wonderful young man. Even without comparing how much he looks like you, I knew it was our boy. Oh, Perry," she said, and reached blindly for him.

He kicked the office door shut as he gathered her into the circle of his arms, gently rocking her back and forth.

"He's a son to be proud of," Perry whispered.

"You're as sure as I am?"

"It has to be. Did you notice that little cleft above his lip—just like mine?"

In agitation, her head moved back and forth on his shoulder. "No. I was so happy that I'd found our son at last that I didn't notice every detail. How can we stand it? We didn't need any more pressure right now."

"But I'm thankful God gave us the opportunity to learn where he is and that he's had a good home. No one can doubt that he's been treated well."

"Only loving parents could have made him as confident and happy as he is." She swallowed a sob before she said, "But after seeing him, my good intentions to never contact our son went glimmering. It's going to be terrible to lose him again after two days."

"I don't intend to lose him," Perry said with determination. "I'm going to tell him that I'm his father."

"Perry, you can't!"

"If he were still a child, I might not say anything to him, but he's a grown man. He may even know we're his natural parents and expect us to speak."

"That isn't likely. Your name wasn't on any of his birth records." Lorene wanted to reveal her identity to Chad, too, but she felt obligated to reject the temptation out of respect for Chad's adoptive parents. "You said before that you only wanted to find out if he needed anything. It's obvious he doesn't need us. If he doesn't know he's adopted, it would be cruel to tell him. Let well enough alone."

Perry knew Lorene was probably right, but he wondered if he had enough self-discipline to keep from claiming their son.

"I won't be impetuous, but I won't promise. We'll see what more we can learn about Chad. He might not be ours. Saunders physical characteristics are strong and they've had a way of passing down through the family for generations. He might have Saunders blood from another family line."

"You're only deceiving yourself—you know he's our son." She pulled away from the warm comfort of his arms. "But I'll have to forget being Lorene Harvey, mother, and become a PR representative again. I still believe it's wrong to enter his life, so I'll put on my business face, smile and make an effort to be impersonal."

He cupped her hand with gentle fingers and kissed her longingly. With the warmth of his lips still on hers, she left the office building and turned toward the chapel. She needed spiritual guidance before she faced Chad again.

Seeking an obscure corner of the room, where she would be unobserved if anyone came in, Lorene knelt beneath a stained-glass-window portrait of Jesus on the cross. Mary, His mother, was on her knees staring up at her son. Rather than emphasizing the agony Christ endured as He died for the sins of the world, the artist had focused on Mary's distress as she watched the death of her child. As she said goodbye to her son Mary obviously felt the pain that Jesus suffered. When His spirit left the physical body and returned to God, He would belong to the whole world.

Staring steadfastly at Mary's face, Lorene identified with the grieving mother. Lorene sensed the pride Mary had in her child—the same pride Lorene had experienced when she'd seen the handsome youth she'd borne. But Lorene also understood Mary's intense sorrow in giving up her son. Lorene believed she'd forfeited any right to be Chad's mother, and that it would be unfair to him, as well as to his adoptive parents, to tell him she was his natural mother. She prayed she'd be able to persuade Perry not to say anything to Chad. If Jon was right, then Chad might be destined to become a pro football star, and as such he would belong to the nation. She had no right to interfere in his life.

But how difficult it would be to see him the next two days and not reveal by word or action that he was more to her than a mere acquaintance! She could understand why Perry was determined to tell Chad that they were his parents. He longed for a son. Would he be content to let Chad out of their lives? Would his longing for a son override Lorene's conscientious conviction that the mistakes they'd made in their youth shouldn't ruin Chad's life now? If the boy was unhappy, she would be inclined to tell him who she was, but Chad seemed to be loved, happy, secure and confident.

"God," Lorene whispered, "I can't do this alone. Giving me the opportunity to see Chad again proves to me that You've forgiven me for giving him up when he was born, and I believe that when You forgive, You also forget. If that's true, You don't even remember what Perry and I did, so I'm not going to fret about it anymore. We've been given the chance to have a new relationship, but we must not build that relationship by destroying Chad's life. Give us strength and wisdom."

Lorene rose wearily from her knees and sat on one of the pews. Through the stained glass, multicolored sunbeams spread around her. She knew what she had to do—she only needed the strength to do it. She would treat Chad as impersonally as she did Preston. And when the concert was over, she'd wave Chad on his way, her professional smile masking the pain that filled her heart, not unlike the spasm of grief that had consumed her when her parents had taken him away from her the first time. Somehow she had to convince Perry that not telling Chad the truth was the right thing to do.

She stopped in the rest room and applied more makeup around her eyes to undo the damage her few tears had caused. She couldn't do anything about the wistful look in her eyes, but perhaps no one would know why it was there.

Chapter Fourteen

As Lorene approached Jon's unmarked van parked near the fountain, she silently thanked God that her parents were no longer in Woodston. If her father had seen Chad and suspected his identity, his reaction would have been unpredictable. But she felt certain that Chad's secret would be safe with her new friends in Woodston. While Chad was the image of his father when Perry had been that age, with the graying hair and mustache, as well as the composure and dignity the years had brought to Perry's face, the relationship of Perry to his son wasn't readily apparent.

Lorene drove the station wagon toward the stadium, with Jon and Chad following her. Zeb's cruiser was parked near the gate, and he leaned against the fence. Lorene lowered the wagon's window, and a puff of hot air warmed her face.

"Hi. Jon Preston arrived early, so he's going to look over the stadium, then go to Stone Gate before the general public knows he's here. Don't advertise the fact that he's already arrived."

"Okay," Zeb assured her. He opened the gate and waved the two vehicles inside, closing the barrier behind them.

"This is a super stadium for such a small town," Jon said with approval when he stepped out of his van and looked around. "My dad was hesitant about accepting this concert, because he figured Woodston wouldn't be able to accommodate us, but we'll have a great time here."

"Woodston's leaders have always built for the future—that's the reason we had lots of information about their past to prepare for the bicentennial. And many people in town expect Woodston to become a large city someday. But, personally, I think they'll be better off to stay as they are. It's a nice family-oriented town."

While Jon joined his technicians to check out the equipment, Chad and Lorene sat on the bleachers. Jon ran through one song to check for volume and clarity, and Lorene turned to Chad.

"He's really good!" she said enthusiastically. "I'd meant to buy one of his CDs and listen to it, but I've had very little extra time the past six weeks. I took over this promotion suddenly, and I've been pressured to get everything done on time."

"You'll have opportunity to get all of his tapes

and CDs this weekend. Two of his songs have hit the top-ten list, and he's only been recording for a year.''

''How'd he get started in the music business?''

''Jon's father taught him to play the guitar when he was a child, and he's been fiddling around with all kinds of instruments ever since. Rather strange that we're such good friends, when we're so different. I can't carry a tune in a bucket.''

The words *Neither can your father* trembled on Lorene's lips, but she smiled and swallowed her sorrow.

''On the other hand, Jon hates sports,'' Chad continued. ''My father was a football player, and he influenced my decision, but Mr. Preston was an amateur musician. Guess we both followed our father's careers.''

Lorene wondered momentarily what Chad would have become if she and Perry had reared him. Would he have been a teacher? Or maybe an engineer?

''Our high school entered a state competition for musical talent, and Jon was the overwhelming choice to represent us. A talent scout from Nashville attended the competition, and he pounced on Jon right away. Mr. Preston is a pretty shrewd guy, and he hired a lawyer and they did a lot of negotiating before Jon signed the contract. Jon's really a shy person, and all of this notoriety is hard on him, but once he picks up his guitar and starts singing, he forgets about his audience.''

Jon joined them, saying, ''Miss Harvey, this is a great place. I assume you made the arrangements.''

''Yes, but at first I wasn't sure there was enough room in Woodston for one of your shows.'' She stood. Chad hopped to his feet and held her arm as they stepped from the bleachers.

''Are you ready to go to Stone Gate? I'm staying there for the weekend, too, and I'll show you the way to the estate. Mr. Peters, the owner, is a senior citizen and a bachelor, so he asked me to be his hostess.''

''I'm sure he couldn't have found a better one,'' Chad said, admiration on his face.

His words pleased Lorene. If he ever learned she was his natural mother, he wouldn't be ashamed of her.

Lorene had surmised that both Chad and Jon were from moderate, middle-class families, and she was sure of it when they stepped out of the van at the entrance to Stone Gate. They stared at the majestic house and the well-groomed landscape in astonishment.

''And we're to spend the weekend in this man-sion?'' Chad finally said. ''Wow!''

''How'd you manage this?'' Jon asked, glancing at Lorene, a besotted grin on his face.

''By having the gall to ask Mr. Peters to let you stay here.''

Reginald came from the house and stood beneath the portico looking as dignified as the house itself.

"Come and meet your host. Reginald Peters is an influential member of the bicentennial commission, and it only took a little persuasion for him to open his home to you. That was fortunate, because there wasn't any other place to house you."

Reginald stepped forward and extended his hand. Dressed in his colonial costume, he could easily have stepped out of the past. Lorene proudly introduced her companions.

"Welcome to Stone Gate, the home of my ancestors," he said. "Come in." Reginald led the way into the large central hallway, where he invited them into the drawing room. "When are the others arriving?" he asked.

"Not until later this afternoon," Lorene said. "Jon prefers to sneak into town and wait until after the concert to greet his fans."

"Good idea," Reginald said.

"I'll check with Mrs. Cossin for some refreshments," Lorene said. "Back in a minute."

Lorene found the kitchen staff in a dither. They hadn't expected anyone before six o'clock.

"Settle down," Lorene said. "These two boys are hardly out of their teens and haven't lived any differently than we have. A year ago Jon Preston was unknown, and I don't think his fame has changed him a great deal."

"We're getting ready for the evening meal, but

what're we going to feed them now? We weren't planning on this," Mrs. Cossin moaned.

"Fix a plate of ham sandwiches, potato chips, cookies and colas from the supplies I ordered for you. You're serving two young men, and they won't want the same food Mr. Peters eats. And as you know, you'll only need a light buffet meal at six o'clock, because Mr. Kincaid has arranged for Jon and his entourage to go on the moonlight cruise of the *River Queen,* where dinner will be served at midnight. They'll have a full meal then."

"Will you tell Mr. Peters that?" Mrs. Cossin pleaded. "He's nearly driving me crazy, coming to the kitchen every half hour to see if we have enough food."

Lorene laughed over this fussy side of Woodston's dignified historian. She'd never seen him with ruffled feathers. "Leave Mr. Peters to me," she said. "Entertaining a celebrity has made all of us a little edgy."

While Jon and Chad took a walk around the estate, Lorene checked all the bedrooms to be sure they were ready for guests. When the rest of Jon's entourage arrived, she supervised settling them into their rooms and encouraged the kitchen staff during the serving of the meal. She liked Jon's parents. She learned from them that Jon was only nineteen, and that they'd given up their own lives to travel with their son until he was older and more sure of himself. Except for his parents, Jon's other associates were people under thirty.

Lorene returned to the apartment to dress for the evening on the *River Queen*. She removed a white silk, sequined, ankle-length dress from its plastic cover and laid it on the bed, then took matching white slippers from the closet. She arranged her hair loosely over her shoulders and applied a light covering of makeup. After she slipped into the sleeveless dress, she debated about what kind of jewelry she should wear, finally choosing a white-gold necklace for the V-necked opening. She fastened long pendant earrings in her earlobes.

She was ready when Perry arrived, now smoothly shaven except for his mustache, and his eyes burned brightly when she opened the door. He stepped inside and handed her a florist's box.

"Oh, I hadn't expected flowers," she said.

"I'm as excited as a boy on his first date," Perry said, an infectious grin spreading over his face. "You look like I should be taking you to your high school prom." His smile faded into a wistful expression. "Something else I missed in your life. I should have been your high school sweetheart, Lorene."

How could she reply to that? She had no answer, so she focused on the corsage. The orchid was beautiful, and she kissed his cheek.

The vivid lavender of the orchid that Perry had pinned to the shoulder of her dress contrasted

sharply with the white dress. His nearness kindled a
flame in the deep recesses of her heart, and the soft
brushing of his fingers unnerved her. When the
flower was in place, he kissed her bare arm and drew
her into a loose embrace to prevent smashing the
corsage.

His white suit, blue shirt and multicolored silk tie
flattered his gray hair and dark eyes. With a catch
in her voice, Lorene said, "I guess this is our first
dress-up party. You look great, Perry."

"Perhaps I shouldn't say it, but we are a handsome couple."

"No harm in telling the truth," she said lightly,
to disguise the unbidden memories that surged
through her body like a tidal wave. "I'm ready, but
I've decided to take along a wrap in case it's cool
on the river." She went into the bedroom to get the
silk lace shawl that had come with the dress.

A light breeze was blowing when Perry parked
his car near the wharf, and they walked toward the
gaily lit boat. The three-deck *River Queen,* small by
comparison to the gaudy, ornate passenger boats of
an earlier era, had a capacity of one hundred. Taped
calliope music, common to the steamboat era,
greeted their arrival. It was easy to feel that they'd
been suddenly transported back to the elegant atmosphere of a sternwheeler of the 1850s. Perry held
Lorene's hand as they crossed the gangplank to the
boat.

"Let's go to the second deck and watch the boat

pull away from the docks,'' he said. To reach the steps, they passed through the elegant ballroom and dining area on the lower deck that was equipped with period furnishings, some of the items genuine antiques. Crystal chandeliers flooded the room with a soft light.

They leaned on the rail, shoulders touching, finding comfort in their closeness. Perry longed to put his arm around her, but they'd seldom shown any public display of emotion, so he stifled his longings again.

As they watched, Jon Preston and his friends arrived at the wharf, and police were hard put to hold back the admiring, screaming fans who surged against the ropes that marked the narrow approach to the gangplank.

''I guess he didn't sneak into town after all,'' Perry said, laughing softly.

Lorene didn't look at Jon. She'd been following Chad's actions as he forcefully but easily picked up two teenage boys and set them on the other side of the barrier.

The crowd continued cheering, and chanting, ''Jon! Jon! Jon!'' until Preston reached the privacy of the boat.

Hearing heavy footsteps behind them, Lorene turned to see Chad approaching.

''Hi,'' he said as he joined them beside the rail. ''I saw you standing up here. Big fun, huh? Woodston is entertaining us in style. I've sure been doing a lot of cool things since Jon became famous.''

"This is a new experience for me, too," Lorene said. "Luxury boats like this often come to Pittsburgh, but I haven't taken a trip on one."

The whistle sounded long and loud, the powerful engines churned to readiness and they felt the gentle pull of the current as the boat left its moorings. A mist from the paddle wheel settled gently on their faces.

"Jon's always shook up the night before a concert," Chad said, "and he thought this trip would be a good way to relax. He didn't know the media had been notified that Jon would be on the cruise."

"Don't blame us," Perry said, throwing up his hands. "The chairman of the commission leaked the news. But we'll be out on the water for several hours, so that should give Jon time to unwind," Perry said.

"I needed to relax, too," Lorene said. "This boat ride is sort of like the icing on the cake. It took a lot of hard work to pull this celebration together, but all of our plans panned out, so it's nice to be able to celebrate."

"After all of this hoopla, Woodston is going to seem mighty dull next week," Perry commented.

"By the way," Chad said, "are you two married?"

Lorene's muscles tensed, but when Perry remained silent, she said, "No. Perry and I were good friends when we were in college, but we went our separate ways and hadn't seen each other until I came to Woodston a few weeks ago.''

"I know you had different last names, but career women don't always change their names now when they marry. I didn't mean to stick my foot in my mouth. It just seems like you were made for each other."

Perry laid an affectionate hand on Chad's brawny shoulder, and they let the subject drop.

Although Lorene and Perry had agreed not to seek Chad's company, after the boat left the dock and was well under way, he followed them into the dining room and asked to sit with them. Lifting his eyebrows slightly in Lorene's direction, Perry requested a table for three. They were given numbers forty-three through forty-five to pass through the buffet line.

As he held Lorene's chair at a candlelit table, Perry said to Chad, "I hope you aren't hungry. This may take a while."

With a laugh, Chad said, "My mother says I'm always hungry, and I'd probably be four hundred pounds if I didn't work out so much."

A waitress took their beverage order and brought a plate of hors d'oeuvres for munching while they waited their turn at the elaborate buffet line. Soft orchestra music blended with the quiet conversation in the room. As Lorene faced Chad across the flickering candles, he looked so much like Perry in his youth that she clenched her hands while grief and despair flooded her heart.

"You said you met in college. Where?" Chad asked, and Perry couldn't help wonder if Chad had an uncommon interest in their backgrounds.

"We were together at Notre Dame until Lorene changed schools," he said. "Her family lived in the Chicago area then, and I came from Iowa."

"I'd have liked to go to Notre Dame. They have a terrific football program, but my folks couldn't afford it. I might have gotten a football scholarship to Notre Dame, but they wanted me to stay closer to home." He glanced at Lorene questioningly. "Didn't you like Notre Dame?"

Lorene spoke with an effort, carefully choosing her words. "My folks moved back East, and I finished college in New Jersey." Forcing a bright smile, she said, "But that's enough about us. We want to hear about you."

"I've lived in the same Alabama town all my life, next door to Jon's family. My folks gave me a car when I graduated with honors from high school, so I commute to college. I'm in my junior year now."

Lorene did some mental tabulation. That would make him the right age to be her child. She would have liked to know his birthday, but she wouldn't ask.

"Dad started me in sports when I was old enough to play in Little League. I've tried most every sport there is, but football seems to be my thing. Dad and

Mom have always encouraged me." He laughed reminiscently. "Rain or shine, they've never missed a game I was playing in. They were there to pat me on the back if I did well, or to hold my hand if I'd fouled up."

"You're an only child?" Lorene finally asked around the pain in her throat.

"Yes. My mother was middle-aged when I came along, and they didn't have any other children."

Every word Chad said seeded a new pain in Perry's heart, but he was grateful to the Reeces for doing what he should have done. Before the evening was over, Lorene and Perry were well acquainted with this child who had been lost to them as an infant.

As Chad talked, Lorene watched him closely, and each smile, tonal inflection and facial expression reminded her of Perry. For the first time, she doubted her decision to conceal their identity from Chad. Was it fair for Perry not to have the pleasure of claiming his son? If Chad was angry because she'd given him away, he couldn't blame Perry, who'd had nothing to do with the adoption. Would it hurt Chad if he found out he was adopted? Or did he already know?

He'd talked freely about his school years—the sports he'd played, his good fortune to receive a football scholarship to Wallace University and his aspirations to play pro football. But he gave no indication that he'd been adopted.

The boat arrived back at Woodston's docks at two o'clock in the morning, and Perry and Lorene drove through town in silence on their return to Stone Gate.

"We can be proud of him," Lorene said as they approached Stone Gate. Before he answered, Perry parked the car, then took her hand as they walked to the house.

"Yes, I'm proud of him. But he's the man he is today because some other couple did what we should have done," he added bitterly.

Lorene noted a hint of condemnation in Perry's voice, and it put her on the defensive. "He probably turned out better than if I'd tried to raise him by myself. A boy needs a father's guidance. My biggest mistake wasn't giving him up for adoption—it was not coming back to you so we could have raised him together."

Perry squeezed her hand, and his voice was kind, so maybe he wasn't blaming her for what had happened. "You did the only thing you could have done under the circumstances, so don't fret about it. It's hard to tell what my reaction would have been if I'd learned you were pregnant, when I didn't have a job and hadn't even finished college so I could find work. If we'd married then, it's doubtful we'd have been happy. We might not even have been very good parents. I'm not worried about what happened twenty years ago. But what's the right thing to do now?"

"Do you still think we should tell him?"

"I don't know. He didn't give any indication that he knew he was adopted, but that isn't something you'd say to strangers."

"But he doesn't treat us like strangers. I've deliberately avoided him, but he tends to seek us out. Is it the blood tie that pulls him toward us?"

"Possibly," Perry said. "But we must be sure of one thing—if we do tell Chad that we're his biological parents, are we doing it for *him* or for *us?*"

"I agree. We'll have to sacrifice our own selfish desires if knowing would destroy his present happiness and self-confidence. Maybe the best way to demonstrate our love is to stay out of his life."

Still holding hands, they walked up the steps to the portico. Perry used her key to open the door into the dimly lit hallway. Since Preston wanted a lot of rest before a concert, all of his people had gone to bed.

Taking advantage of the silent house and the vacant hallway, Perry gathered Lorene in his arms and held her gently. His mouth covered hers hungrily.

"This has been a wonderful night," he whispered against her lips. "Sort of like a family time, the three of us together. If we're never like this again— we'll have this night to remember. Thank you for giving me a son."

"Can we possibly let him fade out of our lives? I thought I'd never go back on my decision, but I don't know how strong I can be when I have to say goodbye.''

''I don't know the answer, either, but I'm praying that we'll know the right thing to do when the time comes.''

Perry went to the wing of the house and took the back stairs to his room. Lorene walked along the breezeway to the small room off the kitchen where the cook had lived in the days of Reginald's parents. After she hung up the white dress, Lorene sat on the side of the bed and dropped her head to her hands.

The next twenty-four hours would be crucial in her life. By this time tomorrow night, the Preston concert in Woodston would be history, and Chad Reece would be gone—back to his adoptive parents and his football career. Would he ever know that he'd spent the weekend with his biological parents? The answer was up to her, for Lorene believed that Perry would abide by her decision. What should she do?

Before she went to bed, Lorene turned in her Bible to the incident where Luke had written that ''Jesus set His face steadfastly to go to Jerusalem.'' Rejection, humiliation, separation from His loved ones on earth, suffering and death awaited Jesus in Jerusalem, yet He didn't turn aside from the plan laid out for Him before the creation of the world. He had received strength to carry out God's will during the interlude in the Garden of Gethsemane when He'd prayed, ''Not My will, but Yours be done.''

Changing into her thin nightgown, Lorene knelt and leaned her head on the bed. Tonight she faced her own Gethsemane. The decisions she made would affect the lives of many people. Turning her back on her only child would result in a lifetime of separation and suffering. But what would Chad's reaction be if he learned who she was? What opinion would he have of an unwed mother who hadn't had the strength to stand up to her parents, to keep him whatever the sacrifice?

After more than an hour on her knees, Lorene wearily got up and crawled into bed. The path she must follow was plain to her and she faced it steadfastly. Praying for strength to do what she should, Lorene turned on her side and went to sleep.

Chapter Fifteen

Lorene awoke at seven o'clock at the insistence of her alarm clock, dressed in shorts and shirt, checked in the kitchen to be sure preparations were under way for breakfast at eight and started out for a run along Stone Gate's roadway. On her return to the house, she met Jon and Chad jogging. They waved and passed on.

They later joined her for breakfast. Jon always ate lightly on the day of a concert, so this would be his last meal until evening, but brunch would be available throughout the morning for the rest of the group.

An hour before the gates opened for the concert, Lorene went to the stadium to be sure everything was ready. Traffic was already congested and a huge crowd clustered around the gates waiting to enter.

Zeb was directing traffic, and he flagged Lorene down.

"Take this side street to a small entrance at the back of the stadium. We're sending Preston's group that way, too."

"Good turnout," Lorene commented.

"Yeah. It's a big day for Woodston."

Jon was on the improvised stage, checking out the instruments with his band members, so Lorene looked for Andy Preston, Jon's father.

"Is there anything I can do to help?" she asked. "Any changes that need to be made?"

He extended his hand. "Miss Harvey, I don't know how you managed to pull this off in the short time you had. We've never had a show that's operated so smoothly. Usually we have a lot of headaches because the local representatives haven't done their work, but you've anticipated every need we have." He paused, looked keenly at her and said, "Jon needs a good press agent—would you be interested in the job?"

Her bright laugh sounded merrily.

"I'm serious," Mr. Preston continued, and threaded his graying hair with his hands. "I'm Jon's manager because I want to be sure no one takes advantage of him, but this kind of life is all new to me. I was assistant manager of a food market before Jon became a celebrity, and I'm out of my element in show business. We could use you."

It passed through Lorene's mind that if she took this job, she would have an opportunity to see Chad often, but becoming Jon's press agent would require all of her time. If she accepted this offer, how could she fit Perry into her schedule? Excluding Perry from her future plans didn't appeal to Lorene.

She shook her head and spoke to Mr. Preston with sincerity. "I'm certainly honored that you've asked me, but I have to refuse for several reasons. In the first place, I have a publicity agency to run. And there's another position I'm angling for right now, but I'm not sure I'll get it. Although it would be a pleasure, I'd have to rearrange my whole life to become Jon's press agent. You have a fine son, Mr. Preston. I pray that fame won't ruin him, and that his temperament and manner will always remain the way they are today."

"That's the reason I'm sticking close to him," Mr. Preston said grimly. "My wife and I will devote our lives to him until he's more mature. Our other children are all older, and they can take care of themselves for a while."

"I'll follow his career with interest. I'll always remember your positive response to our invitation."

"Woodston has been an important place for all of us. And we'll keep in touch. But promise me that you'll think about joining Jon's staff. The boy's got a great future before him, but he's going to need a lot of guidance. I believe you're the one to do it."

"I'll think about it."

The gates opened, and Mr. Preston moved backstage. Lorene checked to be sure her photographers were in place, insuring proper coverage on the national evening news, before she joined Perry in a special viewing booth arranged for the bicentennial commission.

Lorene hadn't attended a country artist's concert before, and she was amazed at the frenzy and enthusiasm of the multitude of fans sweeping into the stadium. Chad and several bodyguards stood between the audience and the stage, ready to block overzealous fans from jumping to Jon's side as he sang. Zeb had recruited several state policemen to mingle with the crowd so that the mass of people didn't get out of control.

Jon's strong tenor voice resounded through the stadium, and Lorene thanked God for giving such a beautiful talent to a boy who was willing to develop it. Jon sang several country songs of bygone days, many of which had originated in the hills of Kentucky and Tennessee, before he passed on to songs that had been written especially for him. He played a guitar to accompany his singing, but he had a backup band of drums and several stringed instruments. After the intermission, when fans flocked to buy Jon's recently released video, Jon sang a repertoire of hymns. He closed by singing "My Old Kentucky Home," a song that brought the applauding crowd to its feet as they joined their voices in the grand finale.

When Jon came on stage for his last song, Lorene

left the special viewing booth. She needed to get ahead of the departing crowd to oversee the final arrangements for the reception at Stone Gate. Jon would be busy autographing after the show, so she had plenty of time.

She probably needed to calm Mrs. Cossin's nerves more than anything else, for while the caterers were in charge of the reception, the Stone Gate staff was preparing the final dinner. A change had been made in Jon's scheduling, and the Prestons intended to leave by nine o'clock so that Jon wouldn't be rushed to keep his recording appointment in Nashville the next day.

Lorene found everything was in place at Stone Gate for the bicentennial's final event. A local disc jockey had set up his equipment in one tent, and Jon's music would be broadcast quietly during the reception. The caterers had brought in thirty small tables and placed them in the shade of the ancient maple trees that were showing a hint of autumn color. Waiters and waitresses, dressed in black pants and white shirts, scurried around placing white cloths on the tables and preparing the buffet table underneath a large tent. In a few more hours her work for Woodston's bicentennial would be over.

Perry arrived a half hour before the reception was scheduled to start. "Need any help?" he asked Lorene.

"Just pray that everything will be all right," she said anxiously. "I can't think of anything we've overlooked. Everything else has gone on schedule, and I don't want any mistakes now."

"How much do you have to do this evening?"

"Not much. The caterers are taking care of the serving. I'm going to station myself out in the gazebo where I can oversee the activities and be available if I'm needed. I'm just the hired help, you know."

"Some hired help," he jeered lightly. "You've been the lifesaver of this celebration, and I think everybody knows that. Mr. Preston was praising your abilities to everyone."

She smiled. "He *did* seem to be impressed with me. He asked me to become Jon's press agent."

A wave of apprehension spread through Perry's body. He'd been anxiously waiting for the celebration to end so he and Lorene could have a serious talk about their future. With a sinking heart, he realized that life in a laid-back town like Woodston would compare poorly to the glamour of promoting Jon Preston's skyrocketing rise to fame.

Trying to mask his uneasiness at this unexpected hurdle, he forced himself to answer noncommittally, "That sounds like a great opportunity for you. Are you interested?"

She was totally bewildered by his reaction. For whatever reason, he'd asked her to marry him. Didn't he realize that if she tied herself to Jon's rising stardom, it would monopolize her life? Or didn't Perry want her any longer?

"Interested enough to tell Mr. Preston I'd think about it."

An uneasy silence built between them. Lorene shook her head to erase the confused thoughts and feelings that harried her. Fortunately, vehicles started arriving in large numbers. Volunteer attendants guided them to a newly mown hay field below the mansion for parking.

The receiving line formed on the front lawn of the mansion. The commission had agonized long over who should be chosen as greeters, but good sense prevailed when it was agreed that only Mr. Kincaid and Reginald, representing Woodston, would stand beside Jon and his parents.

"You go and mingle," Lorene said to Perry. "I'll supervise everything from the gazebo if you need me. That's a good place for me to keep an eye on things."

The gazebo proved to be a pleasant place to watch the progress of the reception. Besides two white benches, there was a swing where Lorene sat, and it soothed her nerves to hear doves cooing softly in the dovecote above her head as she swayed gently in the swing. An hour into the reception Chad and Perry came to join her, carrying three plates of food.

"We decided you were being neglected," Chad said. "I brought you some munchies."

Lorene scooted over to make room for Perry in the swing, but Chad sat on the floor, leaned against a post and thrust his long legs in front of him.

"I'm bushed," he said, looking at Lorene with admiration. "How do you keep up the pace you do and still look as unruffled and beautiful as ever?"

Flattered, Lorene said, "Makeup, hair spray and expensive clothing help."

"This has been a strange weekend in some ways," Chad said reflectively. "It's almost as if I've entered a different world for a few days, like we're living in the past. The people here are so friendly and relaxed—not what we generally find in the cities. Some places, we need extra bodyguards to form a human shield around Jon, but nobody got pushy today. I suppose this lifestyle would get boring after a while, though, and I can't wait to get back to playing football."

"Will your injury keep you on the bench during the season?" Perry asked.

"No. I had some cracked ribs, but they're almost completely healed now. I should be able to play in a couple of weeks. I'm leaving Jon after today, and I'll be back in school on Monday. I only work with Jon when it doesn't interfere with my school schedule."

"What about grades?" Perry asked. "Do you have any trouble keeping up with your studies and still traveling with the football team?"

"No. I've carried a 3.8 GPA average. I was 4.0 all the way in high school, but I've had some tough classes in college."

Perry wanted to know as much about Chad as

possible, and he knew Lorene did, too, and since Chad was in a talkative mood, he questioned him further.

"I've gathered you'd like to play pro football, but what are you studying in college?"

"Electronics and computer science. My parents don't want me to make a career of football, but they know that's what I want. They don't oppose me, but Dad insisted that I get a good, solid education, in case the football thing doesn't pan out."

"Sounds like you have good parents," Lorene said.

"Yes, I have, and I'm thankful for them." He looked at Lorene, his dark eyes unfathomable. "Actually, I'm an adopted kid. I don't know the details, but apparently my adoptive parents couldn't have children of their own, so I'm all they have. I probably appreciate them more than I might have if I'd been their biological son. It means a lot to know that they *wanted* me. I made up my mind a long time ago that I wouldn't disappoint them."

"And I'm sure you haven't," Lorene said softly.

"Do you know anything about your biological parents?" Perry said, hoping Chad didn't note the tremor in his voice.

Chad shook his head. "I've never asked any questions, figuring they'd tell me what I needed to know. Oh, I'll admit there have been times when I've wondered about the circumstances of my birth, and occasionally when I've seen a woman that appealed to me, I'd wonder if she could be my mother. But I've never been curious enough to find out.''

''I'm sure that's a wise decision,'' Lorene said. She looked at her watch. ''This reception is supposed to end in fifteen minutes, and the guests don't look like they have any intention of leaving.''

''It's been beautiful weather for the celebration,'' Perry said. ''We've been fortunate—rain is predicted for tomorrow.''

Chad stood and took Lorene's plate. ''I'd better go see if Jon needs guarding,'' he said. ''I've sure enjoyed meeting you two. I hope I can see you again. Perhaps you could come to one of my games.''

''We'd like that,'' Perry said, and watched silently as Chad's long strides carried him away from them. Casting a side glance at Lorene, he said, ''I believe he'd be angry if we tell him who we are, but, Lorene, I want him,'' and he added through gritted teeth, ''I want my son.''

''So do I, but we can't have him,'' she said bluntly. ''I spent a long time on my knees last night, asking God's guidance about revealing ourselves to Chad. I received the overwhelming conviction that we must stay out of his life. I'm convinced of God's will in the matter, so I'll have to accept it.''

''You act as if you don't even care,'' Perry said through tight, grim lips, and the expression in his eyes was hard and resentful.

She bit her lips at his words and her sense of loss

was beyond tears. She got up from the swing to leave the gazebo. On the bottom step she turned, and her eyes clouded with visions of the past as she observed Perry's stony face.

"Believe what you want to, but remember, this is the *second time* I've lost him."

Reginald Peters stood on the portico, his gray hair shining in the bright light of the moon. Like royalty, he told his guests goodbye and received their thanks for his hospitality. Perry and Lorene stood by the gate and shook hands with them as they came down the walkway.

When Chad reached them, he said, "I'm going to miss you guys. You've been great company." He cuffed Perry gently on the shoulder. "Thanks for being so friendly to me—you've been almost like an older brother this weekend. I've always wanted a brother to lean on. Maybe I oughtta adopt you," he said jokingly.

"That's all right with me," Perry said evenly.

Chad turned to Lorene. "I told you this afternoon that sometimes when I've seen a woman I especially liked, I've wondered if she might be my real mother. I had that feeling the first day I saw you, and I want you to know I've never seen a woman I'd rather have for my real mother."

Perry wondered how much it cost Lorene to smile and say, "Why, Chad, that's the nicest thing anyone has ever said to me! If it's God's will, someday you will find your birth mother, but always remember, your *real* mother is the one who's given you a lifetime of devotion, love and caring.''

"I realize that, but I wanted you to know why I'll never forget you.''

He pulled her awkwardly into his muscular arms and kissed her cheek. His eyes were moist when he turned away.

A smile on her face, Lorene waved the Preston entourage down the driveway, but her heart was bleeding. Sobs rose in her throat as she recalled the heartbreak she'd experienced when Chad was practically snatched from her arms as an infant. Although she'd thought God had been gracious in allowing her to see her son again, now she wasn't so sure. Through the years she'd built a veneer around her heart to counteract the longing to hold her son. Since the day of Chad's birth, she'd never held another baby. When she'd returned his awkward embrace, the protective shield around her heart had shattered. She would suffer this pain of separation as long as she lived.

She turned to Perry, needing his comfort more than she'd ever needed it in her life. She stretched her hand to him, but it fell limply to her side when she observed a swift shadow of rage sweeping across his face. She felt weak and vulnerable in the face of his anger. He opened his mouth to speak, but suddenly wheeled and walked away from her.

Chapter Sixteen

Perry drove away from Stone Gate at a reckless speed, aghast that he'd been on the verge of giving Lorene a tongue-lashing. For two days his heart had identified with the father of the biblical prodigal son, who'd welcomed his long-lost son, saying, "For this my son was dead, and is alive again; he was lost, and is found."

Since Lorene had told him about their child, he'd looked forward to the day when they'd welcome him home as the biblical father had done. When Chad had entered their lives two days ago, Perry had still hoped that Lorene would relent and tell Chad who they were, but he'd given up hope when she'd said she'd prayed for an answer and that God had said to let him go. He couldn't pit his desires against God's will.

When Chad had boarded the bus, Perry had experienced a sense of loss that compared to the way he'd felt when Lorene had deserted him twenty years ago. In spite of himself, his sorrow and hurt had turned to rage against Lorene. She'd caused all of this by running out on him. Although he'd thought they could still be married, now he wasn't so sure. If every time he looked at her, he saw the woman who'd given away their son, could they ever have a happy marriage?

Perry drove blindly, not even realizing where he was until he crossed the river into Indiana. He pulled into the parking lot of a restaurant to orient his mind. Until he settled his emotions, he shouldn't be driving. He couldn't focus on operating a car safely while his mind was so confused.

When his hands no longer shook and his head stopped pounding, he drove back to Kentucky and traveled down the road along the river until he came to Frontier Park. He wondered if this was the place to be if he wanted to put thoughts of Lorene from his mind. In fact, there would never be any place in Woodston he could go now that wouldn't remind him of Lorene, because in the two months she'd been here her personality had touched every corner of the town.

When he pulled into the parking lot behind the fort, he stopped the car and bowed his head on the steering wheel. *God, I've always heard that some prayers are better answered with a "No." Now I believe it. All of those years when I prayed that*

*You'd bring Lorene back to me, for my own good
You were trying to spare me the heartache of knowing about my son. But I thought I knew better what
was good for me than You did, and so I persisted.
Seeing her again has brought me more distress than
I had when I lost her the first time. God, I never
thought the day would come when I didn't want Lorene. Now, after wanting her for so long, it's like
my whole purpose for living is gone.*

Perry stepped out of the vehicle and breathed
deeply of the cool, damp air. Except for a few city
workers cleaning up debris left by the week's visitors, the park was deserted. Wisps of fog drifted in
from the river, and the murky rays of the security
lights reflected on the fort. With no sounds except
the drone of insects and the shifting leaves moved
by a gentle breeze, he thought that the area could
easily have looked like this two hundred years ago.

Perry paused to survey the fort. He tried to en-
vision the pioneers as they'd gone about their daily
tasks, but all he could see was Lorene in her pioneer
garb. Lorene guiding tourists through the area. Lorene bringing food and drink for the artisans. Lorene
sitting by the fire looking at him with compelling,
magnetic eyes that drew him like a lodestone. Eyes
that were filled with a deep longing for their youthful relationship.

Perry settled on a bench along the riverfront, hearing the gentle lap of the current against the bank,
but staring with eyes that couldn't see the present—

only the past. He'd lived almost forty-two years, and Lorene had been a part of his life for about two years of that time. Only a few months when compared to the rest of his years, but during that time had they formed a bond that could never be broken? When she left tomorrow, if he never saw her again, would he face empty years of loneliness? He *would* be lonely, because he knew that no one except Lorene could fill the void she'd left.

"Mr. Saunders," one of the workers said, and Perry started. He'd forgotten that he wasn't alone. He turned toward the man.

"We're ready to leave. I'm supposed to lock the gate."

"I'll lock up for you. I'll be leaving shortly anyway, but it's been a busy week, and I needed to be alone to unwind."

The man handed Perry a padlock. "Sure been a great week, though. Woodston's never had such a party, and that Miss Harvey brought it on. She's a good fixer."

"Yes, she is at that. Good night."

As the workers drove away in the utility truck, Perry stood up wearily. The chill of the night and the dampness from the river pressed upon him, and he shivered. As he turned toward his car, he heard a flutter behind him and watched a small gray-brown bird light on the rail fence that surrounded the stockade. The shrill cry of *whip-poor-will, whip-poor-will* identified the bird.

Whippoorwills usually sang in the spring during nesting time, so why was this one singing on the eve of its southward migration? Was he crying for his mate? When he was a child, Perry had read a legend relating that if the whippoorwill had lost his mate during the summer, sometimes it sang in the fall trying to find her again.

For twenty years Perry had cried for the mate he'd lost, and now that he'd found her again, why did he have to punish himself and Lorene by not forgiving her? When it boiled down to the nitty-gritty, the only mistake had been their precipitous intimate relationship. After that, they'd been victims of circumstances—circumstances mostly orchestrated by Lorene's parents. Why couldn't he forgive Lorene as Jesus had forgiven those who'd wronged Him?

And considering the way Chad had turned out, he doubted that he and Lorene could have reared him any better. As he locked the gates of Frontier Park and drove toward Woodston, once and for all he renounced past mistakes and looked toward the future—a future with Lorene, but without Chad. They had a lot of hurdles to overcome, but if she was willing to marry him, it would work out. He said a final goodbye to his son—for some reason that was a part of God's plan. He'd known Chad only two days, surely not long enough to develop a love for him that could compare with the one he'd nurtured for Lorene during many years.

Although he'd renounced his love for Lorene

when he entered full-time Christian service, he believed that wasn't a sacrifice God required of him. Purposefully he headed for the B and B. He didn't intend to let any more time elapse until he'd made his peace with Lorene. But he looked at his watch— three o'clock in the morning. Lorene would be sound asleep now. After waiting twenty years he could wait a few more hours, he thought, and he turned back into Woodston.

Lorene had readily recognized the expression of contempt and anger on Perry's face when he turned away from her. Alarm and wrath fluttered along her spine, causing her to momentarily forget the loss of her son. How dare he desert her again! Both times when she'd had to endure the loss of her child, Perry wasn't at her side. Fury was churning her insides, and she longed to lash out at someone. Then Reginald appeared at her side.

After all he'd done, she couldn't snap at him. She took a deep breath, forced a smile to her lips and said, "Today has been the crowning glory of the whole celebration. I've promoted a lot of big deals that flickered out at the end like a dud firecracker. But that isn't the way with Woodston's bicentennial. Thanks so much for opening your home for this occasion."

Reginald extended his hand. "And thank you, Miss Harvey. You've put Woodston on the map."

She laughed softly. "Oh, I don't know about that!

I hope I didn't do my job so well that Woodston loses its relaxed charm.''

"I don't think it will," Reginald said with his rare smile. "Woodston has passed through many crises in its two centuries, and a week of notoriety won't change it."

"Thanks again," Lorene said, pressing his hand. "I've made arrangements with all of the caterers to have everything off your property by daylight. I'll check in a few days to be sure that everyone has lived up to their contract."

"And when are you leaving Woodston?"

"Tonight."

The words startled Lorene as much as they did Reginald. She'd had no idea of leaving for a few days, but now she knew that was what she must do. She didn't want to encounter Perry again—especially since it was obvious he was through with her.

"Tonight!" Reginald protested. "You shouldn't start a long trip like that when you've had such a strenuous week. Surely you can wait until morning."

"I'll see how I feel when I get to my apartment and pack my car, but a long drive might blow the cobwebs out of my mind. Besides, staying in Woodston was an interlude I hadn't planned on, so I have lots of work waiting for me in Pittsburgh."

Reginald lifted her hand and kissed it, reminding Lorene of an eighteenth-century cavalier. "We should have made you an honorary citizen of Woodston so you'd stay. Don't forget to keep in touch with us.''

The personal things she'd brought to Stone Gate were already packed in the station wagon, so she walked out to the field that had been full of cars a few hours earlier. Her car was one of the few left, and she noticed in particular that Perry's car was gone.

The lights were still on in the Montgomerys' quarters when she arrived, and she hoped Dottie and John wouldn't go to bed for another hour so that she could say goodbye. She quickly packed her luggage and carried it down to the car, intending to be ready to go before she told Dottie she was leaving.

With checkbook in hand, Lorene knocked on the door that opened into the Montgomerys' private apartment.

''Come in and have a cola,'' Dottie said when she came to the door, wearing shorts and walking barefoot. ''We're tuckered out, and you must be, too.''

Lorene stepped inside the door. ''I want to pay the balance of what I owe you. I'm loaded and ready to leave for Pittsburgh.''

Dottie's mouth dropped open. ''You're not!''

''My work at Woodston is finished, and I need to go back to my business.''

''Kinda sudden, isn't it?'' Dottie peered keenly at her, and Lorene wondered how much her face revealed. As drained and lifeless as she felt, her unhappiness must be apparent to anyone as perceptive as Dottie.

"I know the weekly rent, of course," Lorene continued, "but I haven't kept track of my meals."

"Come into the office," Dottie said. She padded across the porch and into the central dining room, accessing the office behind it. Checking the computer screen, she said, "Add forty dollars for your meals."

Lorene wrote out the check and handed it to her.

"Thanks, Dottie. You and John have been great to me."

"Why don't you wait until morning?" Dottie said. "You don't look up to an all-night drive."

"I'll be fine. If you're ever up Pittsburgh way, stop in and see me." Forcing a smile, she said, "My B and B isn't up to yours, but I can make you comfortable."

Dottie put her arm around Lorene's shoulders, an affectionate gesture that threatened to undo Lorene's composure.

"What's happened, Lorene?" she said compassionately. "I'd like to help."

Biting her lip, Lorene said with effort, "It's time for me to leave."

"When are you coming back to Woodston?"

"Maybe when you have your tricentennial," she said, attempting a joke.

Hesitating, Dottie finally asked, "Does Perry know you're leaving?"

Lorene didn't answer, and when she moved away from Dottie's comforting hand, the other woman grabbed her in a bear hug.

"You come back to Woodston, you hear? I'll provide a week's free lodging."

Lorene took time to tell John goodbye, and thank him for his gracious hospitality. Then she scurried toward her station wagon as if an enemy nipped at her heels. She hoped she'd hidden her misery from her landlady's keen eyes, but when Dottie called after her, "You're making a big mistake," she knew she hadn't fooled Dottie at all.

Was she making a mistake? The question persisted all during the long night hours as she doggedly drove northward. She wouldn't let her thoughts dwell on how Perry would feel when he learned she was gone. The only thing that kept her from turning back was the fear that he was through with her and would probably be relieved to find out she was no longer in Woodston.

At daylight she pulled into the parking lot of a fast-food restaurant and settled back for a short nap. She ate breakfast in the restaurant and took to the road again. She arrived at her home by ten o'clock, which was a fast trip for a woman who couldn't keep her mind on the driving. Lorene had intended to telephone the office, but she had to rest.

Shadows had deepened under her eyes, and her back ached between her shoulder blades. She breathed a silent prayer of thanks that she'd arrived safely—it had been a foolish thing to do, and the farther she'd gone from Woodston, the more convinced she'd been that she should have stayed the night to sleep before such a long drive. Considering her depression and fatigue, it hadn't been safe for her to be on the road. And she kept having the guilty feeling that she'd run out on Perry again.

Lorene disconnected her telephone, in case one of the neighbors tried to call, and fell across the bed without undressing. She awakened four hours later with such a crick in her neck that she cried out in pain when she sat up. After she took a shower and changed into jeans and a sweatshirt, she telephoned Opal and reported that she'd be at work the next morning.

"You've got a stack of mail on the desk more than a foot high, so be sure to take your vitamins," Opal said. "It'll take a week for you to catch up, so you're going to need all the energy you can get."

"I'm used to working. Thanks for taking care of things while I've been gone," Lorene said.

"Reports are great on the Woodston project, so you've pulled off another good one. Congratulations!"

"Thanks. See you in the morning."

Yeah, she'd pulled off another good one, Lorene thought. Such a good one that she'd probably ruined her last chance for happiness. And it *would* be ruined without Perry. After she'd gotten over her quick anger that he couldn't understand why it wasn't right for them to interfere in Chad's life, her heart had been heavy because Perry could never have the son he wanted so much.

Keeping busy so she wouldn't have time to think, Lorene unloaded the station wagon. That accomplished, she went to the post office to pick up her mail and stopped at the grocery store to stock her kitchen cabinets. When she got home, she ran the sweeper and dusted.

It would take all evening to sort through the huge accumulation of mail—mostly junk mail, because she'd had her first-class letters forwarded to Woodston. Before she started on that, Lorene put on her running shoes and exercised along a familiar route in a quiet neighborhood.

When she entered her driveway after the three-mile run that had done wonders for her body's stiff joints but nothing to ease the pain in her heart, she took a deep breath of utter astonishment. Perry's car was parked behind her station wagon, and he was leaning against the porch, waiting for her. The pain in her heart disappeared in a flash.

Mixed feelings surged through her—surprise, confusion, embarrassment, uneasiness—but more than anything else, she experienced an absurd sense of happiness.

Still breathing deeply from her exertion, she gasped, "What are you doing here?"

"To find out why you left Woodston without telling me. You promised you'd never do that again."

"That's not quite what I promised. I told you I wouldn't leave without telling you where I was. You obviously knew my whereabouts, since you followed me so quickly. I haven't been home more than eight hours."

"Why did you leave?"

"After that look of anger and contempt on your face when we told Chad goodbye last night, I didn't think you'd want to see me again. I figured you hadn't forgiven me for giving Chad away, and that you never would. If that was so, I had no reason to stay."

"Well, I've forgiven you for *everything,* so are you going to invite me in?"

She fished a key out of her pocket and opened the door into the kitchen. He followed her inside, closed the door behind him and, putting his hand to her waist, drew her close. Her arms encircled him as she locked herself into his embrace. He pressed his mouth to hers, and she trembled at the sweet intensity of his kiss. He lifted his lips, his breath warm against her face, and she buried her face on his chest while he smoothed her hair.

"Lorene, we've wasted half of our lives in confusion and misunderstandings. Why can't we stop worrying about the past, admit we love each other, get married and take each day as it comes? I can't spend another day without you."

She grinned impishly at him. "If that's a proposal, I'll accept."

"It's a proposal, and I intend to get married before I leave Pittsburgh. I know you can't drop everything and come with me to Woodston on a moment's notice, and I can't move to Pittsburgh now either, but I don't intend to leave here until I put a ring on your finger and you say, 'I do.'"

"I want to marry you. We can surely balance my work with yours, but it won't be easy."

"I make a rather high salary, and I've saved a lot of it. I can afford to support a wife."

"I'm not sure I'd want to stop work, but we'll see. I'm determined that circumstances won't separate us again. I still love you, Perry, perhaps even more than I did when we were younger."

"Same here," he assured her, "so it isn't lack of love that's keeping us apart. Isn't there an old adage that says, 'Love will find a way'?"

"I don't know," she whispered, lifting her lips to his, "but I believe it will. We'll have to be patient."

"I've about run out of patience," Perry said softly, and he kissed her again with a stirring intimacy that caused her heart to soar with happiness.

"Driving up here, I realized that for the past two months we've been acting like a couple of kids. It's time we stopped this misery and got married."

She twisted out of his arms. "Suits me, but we can't get married tonight. I'm thirsty after running, and you probably could use some refreshment, too, after that long drive. What do you want—iced tea or a soda?''

"Anything—just as long as it's cold." He took off his jacket, hung it over the back of a chair, sighed and sat down. "I am tired," he admitted. "More from emotional fatigue than anything else. Now that you've agreed to marry me right away, I realize I'm hungry. Let's go eat."

"I'll prepare dinner here," she said. "I can have grilled steaks, French fries and salad ready in a hurry. And I have ice cream for dessert."

"Sounds like a feast. I'm famished."

While she worked at the stove and he washed the salad, Perry confided, "I thought of possible plans all the time I was traveling. If you want to stay in Pittsburgh, I probably wouldn't have any trouble finding an opening at a college in this area. Or if all else fails, I can fall back on my engineering degree."

"I can operate a PR agency anywhere, too, so let's not make any decisions tonight. I like the idea of just getting married without any 'ifs and buts.' We can shuttle back and forth between Pittsburgh and Woodston until we see what works best for us. Both of us have several options."

"I'll agree to anything as long as we're married and I know you're mine."

While she cleared away the dishes and started the dishwasher, Perry drove a few blocks to check in at a motel.

Later, when they snuggled on the couch in her living room, Perry said, "I'm sorry for running out on you when you must have been hurting terribly to see Chad leave. But I was nursing my own pain, and that kept me from thinking of you."

"It nearly broke my heart when Chad said he'd never seen anyone who'd make a better mother, but I'd asked God for help and wisdom, and I wasn't the one speaking. God chose the words and put them in my mouth, so they had to be what He wanted me to say. It was right to let him go. I have to believe that!"

"Although Chad obviously was drawn to us, he doesn't need us. It would be wrong to interfere in his life now."

"I'm grateful to the Reeces for giving him such a good life. We have to consider them, too."

With a wry smile, Perry said, "I guess being a big brother is better than nothing."

"Does he suspect we're his parents?"

"I don't think so. But the natural blood tie is strong. He feels the pull, but as of now, I don't believe he knows why. Especially after the way you handled the situation."

"I wonder if we'll ever see him again."

"If so, he'll have to take the initiative. He's old enough now to look for his biological parents if he wants to." Perry yawned and closed his eyes. "I've never felt my forty-plus years as much as I do right now. This week has been strenuous."

Lorene stroked her fingers along his forearm. "And as for a child, you know it isn't too late for us to have a family. Lots of couples wait now until they're older and financially secure before they have children. After Hannah in the Bible gave away her first son, Samuel, into the service of God, He blessed her with several more children."

His eyes popped open, fatigue forgotten. "You'd be willing to start a family?"

"Yes, I would. I moaned and groaned a lot about turning forty, considering it an over-the-hill birthday, but I've thought of another adage that better fits my situation. 'Life *begins* at forty.'"

"And so it does! If having children is a part of God's plan for us, then we'll have a family. But more than anything, I intend to accept His chosen will for us. I love you, Lorene, in case I forgot to mention it."

She ran a tempting finger across his lips. "You did say something about that, but it's good to hear it again. But we shouldn't consider the past twenty years as wasted—we'll be even more thankful for a happy marriage because we had to wait so long to have each other."

"Wish I had an engagement ring to make this official."

Lorene extricated herself from his arms. "Just a minute," she said, a mischievous sparkle in her eyes. When she returned, she carried the promise ring Perry had given her when they'd first realized they wanted to be married. She dangled it in front of Perry's eyes.

He sat upright. "You still have it! Does it fit?"

Lorene felt as if she'd had a perpetual grin on her face all evening, and it widened. "I can still get it on, but it's a little snug."

"I even remember what I said to you when I gave you this ring," Perry said, as together they slipped the ring on the third finger of her left hand.

Perry's voice broke with huskiness as he repeated from memory, "I love you with all my heart, and I want to marry you as soon as I possibly can. God made us for each other, and I'll never marry anyone except you."

"Those words mean more to me now than they did the first time you said them."

"No more running away from me?" Perry asked, his black eyes teasing and glowing with happiness.

"No. This time it's 'till death do us part.'"

Their gazes held, and her heart turned over in response to the warmth in his eyes. They shared an intense physical awareness of each other, but they'd once been impetuous in their relationship and lived to regret it.

So, reluctantly, Perry stood and tugged on Lorene's hand until she stood beside him. With his arm around her waist, they walked to his car.

"Tomorrow?" he asked, watching her intently.

"Tomorrow! It takes three days to get a marriage license in Pittsburgh," she said, "but we can cross the border into a neighboring state and get married in one day.'' A tingling sensation started in the pit of her stomach and soon spread over her whole body. ''I've waited for you a long time, Perry, but you're worth the wait.''

As she watched him drive away, an indefinable feeling of rightness engulfed Lorene. Shadows from the past no longer dimmed her happiness.

Epilogue

A year later, Perry and Lorene entered the stadium of a Kentucky school hosting Alabama's Wallace University in the conference championship football game. During the year they'd had occasional notes from Chad, and he'd even telephoned once, delighted to find out that they were married.

They'd been careful to let him pursue the relationship. A month ago he'd sent them tickets for this championship game—a game that might get Chad into the pro draft. He'd written a short note.

"It would mean a great deal to me for you to be at this game. My parents will be there, too, and I'd like you to meet them."

Perry followed Lorene as she wound her way through the excited crowd. A couple sat to the left of their reserved seats, and Lorene said, "I'm Lorene Saunders, and this is my husband, Perry. Are you Chad's parents?''

The man stood. "I'm Stewart Reece, and this is my wife, Betty. We're glad to meet you. Chad talks often of the good time he had in Woodston when he met you.''

Betty Reece was a reserved person, and although she made an effort to be friendly, Lorene thought the woman seemed a bit nervous. Of course, it might be nothing more than the anxiety of meeting strangers.

The Reeces were probably in their early sixties, of fair complexion and blue eyes. No one would ever think that they were Chad's natural parents.

The Wallace team surged out on the field amid the cheers of hundreds of fans who'd traveled miles to cheer their team to victory. Before the game started, Chad spared a glance in their direction, and Lorene and Perry lifted their hands. He smiled, obviously happy that they'd come to watch him play.

The game was a thriller from start to finish. The two teams were equally matched, and the score seesawed back and forth. With a minute left in the game, the score was 31-28 for Kentucky. While the fans noisily cheered for their respective teams, the Kentucky running back took a hard shot and fumbled the ball. The Wallace defense recovered the fumble.

The Wallace quarterback took the snap from center and found Chad sprinting down the sideline. He threw the ball with all he had and Chad leaped into the air. With the Kentucky cornerback matching Chad's every move, the ball floated between the defender's arms into Chad's hands. The cornerback lost his footing when he landed and Chad slid into the end zone for the winning touchdown.

While the fans went wild and ran out on the field, Lorene and Perry complimented the Reeces on their fine son and prepared to leave.

"We're meeting Chad for dinner to celebrate the victory. He asked me to invite the two of you," Mr. Reece said.

Perry looked at Lorene and, biting her lips, she shook her head imperceptibly. Meeting the Reeces had been almost more than she could bear—she didn't want to prolong the agony.

"We appreciate your invitation, but we need to be back in Woodston for a college function," Perry said. "We'll stay long enough to congratulate Chad, though."

Flushed with victory, Chad grabbed his mother in a bear hug when he came out of the locker room. Lorene tried to curb the stab of jealousy, but it came too quickly, and she only hoped it didn't show on her face. Chad released his mother and threw an arm around his father's shoulder. Then he turned to Lorene and Perry and grabbed their hands.

"Thanks for coming today. I guess I wanted to show off for you a little."

"And you did!" Perry said with warmth. "A great game, Chad."

Chad was obviously disappointed when he learned they wouldn't have dinner with him.

"Maybe I can stop by Woodston to see you over the Christmas holidays."

"I've accepted a teaching position in Southern California," Perry said, "and we're leaving Woodston in a few weeks."

"I don't want to lose track of you," Chad said, obviously disturbed at the possibility.

Lorene took a card from her purse and handed it to Chad. "This will be our new address. If you're ever out on the West Coast, please look us up. We'll want to follow your career."

"I sure will."

"Hey, Reece, get back in here," the coach called from the doorway. "The press wants to talk to you."

"Thanks again for coming," he said. He bent and kissed Lorene's forehead, and she couldn't stop the quivering of her lips when he turned away.

They made their goodbyes to the Reeces and had started toward the parking lot when Perry felt Stewart Reece's hand on his shoulder.

"How about giving us one of those cards?" he said. "Since Chad likes you so much, it seems like a good idea for us to stay in touch. That'll make it easier for you to know what Chad is doing."

Mrs. Reece came to Lorene, and with genuine sorrow in her eyes she gathered Lorene into her arms.

"Thanks for not telling him," Mrs. Reece said, tears streaming over her cheeks.

Lorene started sobbing and, clearing his throat, Perry asked, "How did you know we were his parents?"

It must have been an emotional moment for Mr. Reece, too, for he swallowed several times before he said huskily, "His mother's name was on the adoption papers, and when Chad came home last fall talking about you, we were sure that he'd met his mother. We didn't realize you were his father, but it's obvious, after seeing you today. In twenty years Chad will look exactly like you."

Lorene pulled away from Mrs. Reece and sought comfort in Perry's embrace.

"We've had a miserable year, wondering if you'd tell him who you were," Mrs. Reece said. "But if he suspects anything, he hasn't mentioned it."

Drying her eyes on Perry's handkerchief, Lorene murmured, "It was a great temptation to tell him, but since I'd given him away, I believed I'd forfeited any right to be his mother."

"Someday we'll tell you how this happened," Perry said, "but we must leave now. If Chad sees us like this, he'll wonder why. We're grateful to you for giving him such a great home. I doubt we could have done any better."

Both Perry and Stewart Reece supported weeping

wives as they searched for their cars in the parking lot. When Perry headed their car homeward, Lorene turned to him, and happiness gleamed through the tears in her gray-green eyes.

"God is good," she whispered. "We haven't lost him after all."

* * * * *

Dear Reader,

This morning as I read the Bible, I came across a verse that emphasized an important principle referred to in this book.

"If you do not stand firm in your faith, you will not stand at all." (*Isaiah* 7:9b)

The hero and heroine, Perry and Lorene, experienced many years of loneliness and heartache because they didn't stand firm in their conviction that premarital sex was inappropriate for Christians. "Anyone, then, who knows the good he ought to do, and doesn't do it, sins." (*James* 4:17) My characters went through months of frustration and doubting before they finally realized that God loves and forgives, regardless of the sin.

All of us have difficult choices to make, but the Bible provides guidance for those who want to live righteous lives and stand firm in decisions that would compromise our Christian principles. It's my prayer that those of you who read this book will be encouraged to take a stand whenever you're confronted with a decision between right and wrong. "Therefore put on the full armor of God, so that when the day of evil comes, you may be able to stand your ground, and after you have done everything to stand." (*Ephesians* 6:13)

If we stand for nothing, we'll fall for anything.

I can be contacted at P.O. Box 2770, Southside, West Virginia 25187.

Irene B. Brand

Next Month From Steeple Hill's

Love Inspired®

The Christmas Groom
by
Deb Kastner

In order to escape his unhappy family, Colin Brockman
enlisted in the navy while studying to be a navy
chaplain. He's finally enjoying freedom for the first
time in his life when he meets straitlaced graduate
student Holly McCade. Though they couldn't be more
different, Holly and Colin can't deny their attraction
for each other. Will this mismatched couple prove that
opposites really can make a perfect match?

Don't miss
THE CHRISTMAS GROOM

On sale December 2002